Deeper

Selected Short Stories

Cliff Jackman

Manor House

Library and Archives Canada

Cataloguing in Publication

Jackman, Cliff, 1980-
Deeper : selected short stories / Cliff Jackman.

ISBN 978-1-897453-34-6

I. Title.

PS8619.A224D44 2010   C813'.6   C2010-907092-5

First Edition.
144 pages.
All rights reserved.

Cover design: Michael B. Davie and Donovan Davie
Photo by Barry L McKay, Photographer – aka Franky2step.
We are grateful for the use of Mr. McKay's photo
To contact Mr. McKay email: bmckay@cogeco.ca

Published October 30, 2010
Manor House Publishing Inc.
www.manor-house.biz
(905) 648-2193

We gratefully acknowledge the financial support of the Government
of Canada through Book Fund Canada, Dept. of Canadian Heritage.

Manor House Publishing Inc.
www.manor-house.biz
905-648-2193

Table of Contents:

1 Escape to Parry Sound

Life is what happens when you're busy making other plans.

John Lennon

All his life Mitch had felt as if he was missing something, something really good. Even after he was much too old for such things, he'd escape into juvenile daydreams in which he'd become famous for some vague reason and had met beautiful actresses and attended glamorous parties.

His own family felt somehow unreal. He could never remember having looked at his wife without noticing some flaw and he'd married her for the same reason he'd taken over the business; because she was there, and because it always seemed like the easiest thing to do. He loved his children but he always thought that he didn't feel what other fathers felt about their children. They were a constant source of surprise to him; he was never able to figure out what they were about to do, or get comfortable around them.

Perhaps it was this tendency in him, to see the problems in everything, that allowed him to recognize what was coming so much earlier than everyone else. And so he took the money out of the business and had the shelter constructed underneath the family's cottage on Lake Muskoka. Shelley complained, of course, and when he persisted she started making cracks about it to their friends and relatives, trying to make him look like a kook. It didn't matter. It was something he had to do.

And when things started to come to a head, he gathered up his imperfect family and shepherded them out of the city. They watched things get worse and worse on television until one evening he told everyone that he wanted them to sleep in the shelter that night. By then the pitch of hysteria in the media had grown so high that they were grateful to him for being the one to take the strange burden of assuming the worst.

Three nights afterwards it started. It was all very unreal listening to it happen underground. The news reports were first hysterical, than tightly circumscribed and clipped. They went through a brief phase where they were oddly conversational and religious before switching to a repetitive, pre-recorded message. After about seven weeks, they just stopped, and there was nothing but silence on every channel.

And so they spent another eighteen months in those cramped rooms, gradually going through the supplies of tinned goods and the fuel for the generator. Spending many hours in total darkness. They read and they talked and they played games. They did yoga to keep in shape in the limited space. They rarely fought because none of them had the heart.

Eventually, Shelley began to push for them to start heading outside. Mitch steadfastly refused. As far as he was concerned, if there was nothing on the radio, they were better inside than out. There was every reason to believe, based on what they'd heard before the silence began, that the world was poisoned.

But perhaps more importantly, he knew in his heart that if there were any survivors they would not be friendly. He reminded her of the trips they'd taken to the Third World. Morocco, Egypt, Mexico, the Dominican Republic. All those hungry eyes on them all the time.

But their food was dwindling away. They had problems with the generator, and with the toilet. And then, miraculously, they began to hear a message over the radio:

"Attention attention. This is Lt. Col. Albert Ross of the Canadian Forces. All survivors please make your way to the Parry Sound base, located at 28 Waupeek Street, in Parry Sound. We are evacuating Ontario and moving all the residents to the west. Attention attention. Everyone hearing the sound of my voice, please make your way to the Parry Sound base. We are moving everyone out west. Thank you."

It was not a recording; the words changed every time. The voice was rich and deep and self-assured. Upon hearing it, Mitch could sense that it was time to go. This was what he had been waiting for, all along. Rescue. Escape. This was their chance, their moment.

And so he wrapped up his family in Gore-Tex outfits from Mountain Equipment Co-op and gave them hiking shoes. They did up their hoods and strapped breathing filters over their mouths. Then Mitch picked up his rifle and they climbed up the ladder back to the uncertain outside world.

*****

The cottage had been completely ransacked. The windows were shattered and the cupboards were empty. There was dirt tracked through the floor.

Outside it was completely silent. There was not a breath of wind. The lake was as still and silent as water at the bottom of a mineshaft. Dead leaves carpeted the ground. The trees were leaning over at impossible angles. Many of them had already fallen to the ground. The sky was a strange colour, almost green, as if there was a yellowish tint in the air. And the whole world smelt a little off, like a cat's dirty litter box or ancient soiled laundry.

Mitch walked down the road that led back to the Trans-Canada Highway. They soon passed cars stopped in the middle of the road, windows smashed, tires slashed.

"Why'd they break everything, Dad?" Geoff asked.

"What?"

"Why'd they cut the tires?" Geoff asked. "What was the point of that?"

"I guess everyone's just upset."

In truth it made Mitch think about that "broken windows" theory the police had cooked up to fix NYC in the 80's. The idea that if you let people break windows and spray graffiti you created an environment where crime was more likely to take place. And when Mitch looked up at the sky, now turning burnt orange with the afternoon, he couldn't help wonder what men would give themselves the licence to do in a world like this. Under a sky like that.

That night they set up the tent. It was an unnatural shade of blue and it stood out like a sore thumb among the dead trees.

Mitch told his wife that he would wake her halfway through the night, so they could sleep in shifts. Instead he stayed up the whole night, listening desperately for any sound. There was nothing. No crickets, no frogs. Not a breath of wind.

The sky shimmered at night, something like the dark rainbows you might see in a puddle of gasoline spilt on asphalt. It did not get very dark. And the next morning, the sunrise was spectactular - a kind of radiant purple, fading off to orange and yellow at the fringes.

After their breakfast of bars made out of pressed dates and water from the canteens they started making their way north along the highway. Around ten o'clock in the morning (it was difficult to tell). Mitch glanced behind them and saw that someone was following.

"Hey!" he shouted, and raised his rifle.

The man raised his arms. He was short and filthy and he had long hair and a beard. "Don't shoot," he said.

Mitch suddenly realized he didn't know what to do.

The man following them licked his lips. Mitch caught a glimpse of black stumpy teeth and a grey tongue.

"Who are you?" the man said.

"Get lost," Mitch said.

And then he wondered: was this an ambush? A trap. He tried to glance around in all different directions at once. They were out of the woods now and so there didn't seem to be anywhere to hide. But then where had this guy come from?

"Where'd you come from?" the man said. "Where'd you get them clothes?"

He took a few steps forward.

"Get away from my family," Mitch said.

"I just ..." the man said. "Where'd you come from? Are you lost?"

"Leave us alone."

"Where are you going to?"

"We're not telling you anything," Mitch said.

And he wondered: should I kill this man? Just pull the trigger and watch him drop? It was the safest thing to do. He tried to think of a single reason to let this man live and couldn't. So what if the stranger didn't pose a danger? So many people were already dead. Another one wouldn't matter. It couldn't matter at all, in all this.

Perhaps out of force of habit, he didn't do it.

"Get away from us," Mitch said.

"But wait," the man said. "Maybe we should travel together. My name's Jason."

"If you follow us I'll shoot you," Mitch said, and then turned and started walking away, keeping his family in front of him. The fabric of his Gore-Tex pants swished. Every now and then he glanced over his shoulder and he saw that the man was standing in the road, just watching.

Around mid-afternoon they stopped for more snacks.

"My feet hurt," Katie said, whining a little. "How much farther is it?"

"We should get there tomorrow around lunch time," Mitch said.

"How do we know there's going to be people there?" Geoff asked. He was a skinny 10-year-old intellectual with hollow-looking eyes.

"Well, that's what the radio said," Mitch replied. "We couldn't stay in the shelter. Hopefully we'll be able to get a ride out west."

"But what's there going to be out west?" Geoff asked.

"Hopefully that's where the people are."

"What people?"

"You know, where the good guys are. Where there's civilization. It might not be as bad, out west."

Geoff's eyes didn't register much understanding.

"We have to give it a try," Mitch said.

"Why would things be different out west?" Geoff asked.

"There's less people there, for one thing."

"But does that mean it'd be different?" Geoff asked.

"That's enough, Geoffrey," Shelley said, her voice threatening violence.

Mitch looked back the way they'd come and saw that 'Jason' was lurking about eight hundred metres behind them, sitting at the curve of the road.

"Hey!" Mitch shouted, and sprang to his feet. "What did I tell you?"

He raised the gun and quickly jogged towards Jason, who raised his hands and then bolted back into the underbrush. Mitch looked back to his family and worried again about ambushes and hurried back to them.

*****

They made their way through the town of Falding as night was falling. There was nothing but a few houses standing empty and abandoned, broken windows and glass scattered across the street, winking in the fading light. Cars were everywhere. It was amazing how many there were when they stopped moving around. Mitch took his family inside a few houses but there was never anything there. Empty cupboards and more things smashed up out of pure meanness.

That night he debated where they should sleep. Of course, there was something to be said for taking refuge in one of the houses. But if they did, they'd be trapped. Although he couldn't be sure, Mitch thought that Jason was still following them - somewhere out among all the crashed and crumpled cars.

In the end he just couldn't bear the thought of being trapped down there, of hearing the laughter of rapists and cannibals, their footsteps on the stairs. There'd be too much time to think about how he'd fucked up. So they pitched the tent in the woods again and once again Mitch stayed up all night. He wasn't even tired, he felt jazzed up and alert. He felt good. They were only a few hours away from Parry Sound.

That morning it rained. Something about the rainwater was off. It smelt of rotten eggs, or dirty socks. There seemed to be a dank mist rising from the ground.

Parry Sound was in much worse shape than Falding had been. The buildings were burned and falling on top each other. Great holes had been dug in the earth and were filled with jagged remains of various works of man. There were obscenities and blasphemies spray-painted onto the ground, along with oddly haunting references: 'where the light is as darkness', 'lord help us', and perhaps most chilling, simply 'they're coming.'

There was no human activity anywhere, not a soul. Mitch could taste the disappointment in the back of his throat. It felt like this was happening to him for a reason, like it was his fault. He was a failure. It had been his idea to build the shelter, to stay down, and then to come out here. There was obviously nothing to see.

"Where's the base, Dad?" Geoff asked.

"Down by the water," Mitch said. "We'll see what's there."

They walked down to the base and came up to the train tracks. The station loomed to their left; two stories high and dark and abandoned, seeming to sag inwards. Nothing around at all. Not a soul. Still not even one sound.

"Dad," Geoff said.

"What?" Mitch snapped.

And then the arrow hit him, right in the chest. The tip of it poking out his back. The gun bounced out of his startled hands and his knees buckled and he fell back to the ground.

Shelley put her hands to her face and started screaming. Mitch put his hands around the arrow and tried to move it but was hit with a wave of pain that he couldn't believe or understand.

"Dad!" Geoff said, and fell on his knees next to Mitch.

And then a moment later something rushed up on them from the side. It took Mitch a moment to realized it was a human being. Naked and covered with filth, eye jumping out of the face, mouth stretched open in a hysterical grimace of excitement, of adrenaline-fueled ecstacy. He had a club in his hand and he struck Shelley and knocked her to the ground.

Geoff ran, taking off along the train tracks the way they'd come. Someone else chased him while the first attacker grabbed Katie and threw her to the ground.

"No!" Mitch shouted, and tried to get back to his feet. But someone kicked him in the back, close to where the arrow was, and the pain was so great he collapsed to the ground. He stared up at that unearthly orange sky.

*****

There were two of them, both caked in filth, both long-haired and crazy. They bound Mitch's arms behind him, then they pushed the arrow through his shoulder to get it out, while he screamed and screamed.

The interior of the military base looked like it had been gutted by a hell of an electrical fire. It was dark and smelt of urine and something worse. Mitch and Shelley were were stripped naked and their clothes were thrown on an enormous pile.

Their kidnappers did not speak except to issue short commands.

Shelley was whimpering, and trying to shield her nakedness from everyone. Mitch knew what was happening. These were not lustful men. They could not afford such luxuries. Their eyes were shining with one light and one light alone.

"Where's Katie?" Mitch said.

They were dragged downstairs into pitch blackness and left on the cold stone floor. Then their kidnappers tromped back upstairs and left them in the dark.

Shelley started breathing faster and faster, and then went into hysterics. Mitch listened to the sound of it while he bled onto the floor. He didn't comfort her, since he was tied up, injured. Also because there was no point. To him it seemed ridiculous to worry about any of this now. They had been caught. His own stupidity and weakness and failure.

Now Geoff and Katie were god knows where and the rest of them were going to die.

After a while she tried to talk to him.

"How are we going to get out of here?" she said. "We've got to do something! Where's Katie?"

For a while, Mitch didn't answer. In the darkness, perhaps Shelley would think he was dead or unconscious.

"Mitch!" she said. "Mitch! Mitch!"

"Yes," he finally said.

"Where are you?"

"I'm here. I'm right here."

"What are we going to do?"

"There's nothing we can do, Shelley," Mitch said. "We aren't going to get away. They got us."

"How can you say that?" she shrieked. "We're going to die if we don't do something."

"Yes," Mitch said. "We're going to die."

And then she was quiet.

*****

After about a day they came back down. One of the killers was wearing Mitch's Gore-Tex. He thought they would take him but they took Shelley instead. She wailed as they dragged her up the stairs, struggled, fought. It made no difference.

Mitch lay on his face, completely broken, unafraid. Upstairs he heard a terrible thunking noise, and then a long, anguished set of screams.

He moved his hands back and forth, back and forth, under the ropes. He'd been doing so for hours but was unable to get anything to happen. His shoulder was pulsing with pain and the wound felt very warm; it was almost certainly infected.

About an hour after they'd taken his wife his skin broke and he started bleeding all over the ropes. They started to turn slippery, and his skin was slick. He pulled as hard as he could with his good arm and finally his hand popped out of the ropes.

Now Mitch rolled onto his back. He couldn't move his left arm at all but with his right one he picked at the knots that were binding his feet. Sometimes his fingers were too stupid and his mind would get dizzy from lack of sleep and water. In those moments he'd close his eyes and dream he was somewhere else.

Finally the ropes came undone and Mitch managed to stagger to his feet. Miraculously, he didn't fall. The blood swam to his head and he felt dizzy but instead of falling back down he padded over to the stairs and climbed them, using his knees and his good hand, until he came to the door. It was locked, but it felt flimsy.

Mitch leaned back and hurled himself against it, next to the lock. His wounded shoulder bleated out a painful protest but the wood splintered and the door gave way.

Mitch fell to the ground and then stood up again, wavering on his feet. It was marginally less dark and he looked around the dim room for something he could use. Eventually he picked up a chunk of cement and plaster that fit into his hand pretty well and started wandering from room to room in the base.

He walked into the room where the bodies of his wife and daughter were and then retreated quickly around the corner, pressing the back of his forearm against his mouth and feeling his stomach lurch.

"Fuck," he said, "fuck fuck fuck. Oh, no no. Oh no."

And then he shuffled off through the hallways, a broken man.

"Well, I don't care what you say," a voice said, startlingly close. "I know where I left it." The voice was just around the corner, perhaps fifteen feet away.

Mitch could hear something faint and muffled coming from further off.

"Yeah?" the closer voice said. "Well, fuck you buddy. It was sitting right on the table ..."

Mitch bolted around the corner with his hand behind his back. The cannibal had a moment to glance at him and register surprise on his face before Mitch smashed him with the rock as hard as he could, slinging it around from his back, the power of it starting somewhere around his navel, and following through all the way down to the ground.

The cannibal made a sound: "Hep!" and then fell against the wall, bringing his hands against his face and moving slowly. Mitch hit him again, then straddled him, and hit him again. The wound in his shoulder broke open and started to bleed.

"Hey!" someone called from deeper in the house. "What's going on?"

Mitch tossed aside the bloody chunk of plaster and looked over the cannibal (who was wearing Shelley's jacket) for something he could use and found a short, blunt knife in a sheath on his belt. Mitch pulled it out and stood naked as he heard footsteps approaching and then heard the door open to the hallway. Then he sprung and planted the knife directly in the other cannibal's throat. The knife disappeared and the cannibal fell back, eyes wide, bleeding slowly down the front of his chest. Mitch watched him fall over and put his hands on his throat and make a noise like "haaak! haaak!" Then he walked past him into the room.

It was not immediately clear which way to go, or what to do. Mitch walked past the dying cannibal and found some stairs heading upwards. He took them, looking at the cracked and peeling paper on the walls, and the dark patches in the corners of the rooms. Smelling the smell of something whose time was up but had resolved not to go quietly.

And then he heard the voice:
"Attention. Attention. This is Lt. Col. Albert Ross of the Canadian Forces. All survivors please make your way to the Parry Sound base, located at 28 Waupeek Street, in Parry Sound. We are evacuating Ontario and moving all the residents to the west. Attention attention. Everyone hearing the sound of my voice, please make your way to the Parry Sound base. We are moving everyone out west. Thank you."

Very faint. Coming from the other end of the hall. Mitch walked over there slowly. He came to a door and put his hand on the knob.

"Attention attention. This is Lt. Col. Ross of the Canadian Forces. I am speaking for the government of Canada."

And Mitch opened the door.

It was a wide, empty room. What had happened to all the furniture in this brave new world? Far across from him there was a window, and at this window there was a table. A man in a wheelchair was sitting at the table holding a radio transmitter and speaking into it. He was naked and grey and a bow and arrow were resting within easy reach.

"All survivors please make your way ..."

Mitch shuffled towards him, unarmed, without any clear idea of what he was going to do.

The man in the wheelchair picked up his reflection in the glass, stopped speaking. Turned around with the bow and the arrow in his hand. Mitch looked into his eyes and saw nothing more than a mindless and feral determination to keep breathing. He waited to be hit by the arrow.

Then, a loud BANG and the man's head blew apart.

Mitch spun around and saw Jason holding his rifle.

"Got him," Jason said with satisfaction.

"You?"

"Me," Jason said, and walked over to the body to make sure it was dead. "Look at that. He went right in his chair."

"Oh," Mitch said, and looked around for somewhere to sit down. "I don't feel so well."

"Yeah," Jason said. "You're probably infected. You'll be all right now. We'll just have to find some clean water and see what we can do. Those boys'll have some around here somewhere."

Mitch licked his lips.

"How are we going to get out of here?"

"Out of where?" Jason asked.

"Out of ... all this. All this."

Jason looked like he understood.

"Buddy, this is all there is. There isn't anything outside of this. This is the way things are. There's not anything else. It's all there is. Do you get it?"

"Yeah," Mitch said. "I think I finally do."

2 Treading Water

Ah, love, let us be true
To one another! for the world, which seems
To lie before us like a land of dreams,
So various, so beautiful, so new,
Hath really neither joy, nor love, nor light,
Nor certitude, nor peace, nor help for pain;
And we are here as on a darkling plain
Swept with confused alarms of struggle and flight,
Where ignorant armies clash by night.

Matthew Arnold

I'm a Canadian, born and raised in Hamilton, Ontario, and all my life I wanted to be a writer. I ended up going to medical school and practicing for a couple of years before I burnt out. It was pretty ugly; I called my parents and cried on the phone a bunch of times and everything. I guess you could say I had a bit of a nervous breakdown, really.

I gave up my practice and ended up writing a novel, kind of a film noir but a book, if you know what I mean, and I took it to a very prominent editor my cousin knew to try to get it published. The editor liked the book, but he didn't publish it (and isn't that always the way?) but more than that he liked me, or at least took pity on me a little bit, and we talked a few times off and on, until I mentioned that I thought the best book I'd ever written was actually a *Star Wars* novel.

Well, it just so happened that this editor knew someone at Del Rey, and he arranged an introduction. I had a phone conversation where I pitched my idea, basically a gritty political thriller set inside the totalitarian government of the Empire. It was unlike what they normally did. There were a number of phone conversations, a number of pitches. Normally I'm terrible at that sort of thing, but I really believed in the book, and I was able to make my case. Eventually, they decided to go with it, and, well, the rest is history.

The success from the book kind of spring-boarded me into a sweet screenplay gig, adapting one of the most popular video games of all time. I'd done wonders for *Star Wars*, so why not *Half-Life*? Now I had some crazy ideas for that too, only those conversations were a lot harder. Everything you've heard about the idiocy of studio executives is absolutely true, but I managed to get the guys at Valve, the developer of *Half-Life*, on my side, and they helped out a lot. The movie got made my way (more or less) and the rest is history there too.

Since then, I've been working on a number of projects, but I've been finding it difficult. This is because until recently I was, once again, as depressed as shit.

And I bet you're thinking, what the fuck have you got to complain about?

Well, there are little things. I have had some romantic problems last year. I'm not going to get into the details but there was a girl involved with the filming of the movie and I fell pretty hard for her and she fell hard for me, too, at first, but she changed her mind and I didn't. I didn't make a scene or anything, I'm not the begging or stalking type, but I really thought I'd found the one and when it didn't work out I was gutted.

And the movie business. Ugh. You know, you argue with these people, it turns out you're right about everything, so you figure that they'll listen next time. Well, you're wrong. Guess what? Now *Half-Life*'s a big franchise and the studio's counting on it and there's a thousand times more suits on it and they're a thousand times more obstreperous.

But that's not really enough, is it? So what do I really have to complain about?

Nothing, of course. I know it doesn't make sense, but I was (and am) acutely conscious of the fact that I have nothing to complain about at all. But I still feel this aching sense of loss, like something's missing. I still feel so miserable. And that makes me feel two things. It makes me feel impotent and powerless, like I'll never be happy. And it makes me feel alone, because there's no one I can talk to who understands.

*****

Recently, I started talking to myself, even in public, arguing with voices that always seemed to be putting me down. Every now and then I'd cry, for no particular reason. I started calling my parents again, the way I'd done towards the end of my medical career. I love my parents; they never get frustrated with my emotional late night calls (later now that I'm on the west coast), they're baffled but they're always sympathetic and concerned.

After the Eisner Awards at Comic-Con in San Jose at the end of July, I flew back to Canada for a wedding. The groom was a friend of mine from way back, and the service was so lovely, and everyone was so happy, it made my heart glad to see it. But at the same time, I couldn't help feel how far away I was from all that. I felt like a robot with a broken leg, stomping around in a circle, while everyone else marched serenely onwards.

I got drunk on the flight home. I was supposed to be doing a lot of writing. I had to crank out two comics a month, I was behind on my film projects, and I had promised the good folks at Del Rey a sequel to the *Star Wars* book. And of course, don't forget, if I got off my ass and found the time, I was supposed to write another novel, a really good one this time. But I was starting to worry I just couldn't do it. I so rarely have good ideas anymore. I was always adapting this or that, telling a story with characters someone else had made, like a kid playing with dolls.

And I couldn't help but wonder: is this it? This is making it? Jesus Christ, I'm a thirty-six-year-old boy, no wife or kids, getting drunk every weekend and writing stories about Aquaman. Somehow it makes it worse to have an enormous house in Malibu; the only thing that could have given my present situation a shred of dignity was poverty.

So the first thing I did when I got home was to make a very foolish purchase. Specifically, I bought a used Ford GT, one of the limited edition ones that came out a few years ago, for a cool 200 large. It was sold to me by an elderly Jewish man who had a dry cleaning business in Pasadena. He was quite well to do and he had a constantly rotating collection of expensive cars. Apparently his wife wouldn't let him have more than five at a time.

"You like cars?" he asked me.

"Not really," I said. "I think I'm having a nervous breakdown."

He nodded sagely. We were standing on his front yard looking in his garage. He had a can of Old Milwaukee in one of his gnarled hands.

"Well, I can't take it back if you change your mind," he said. "But they only made four thousand and thirty eight of 'em in the whole world. It was a limited edition. You'll be able to sell it if you need to, but you might lose a bit on it."

"That's okay," I said. "Money's not the problem."

The old man looked me in the eye and smiled, a little sadly. "It never is," he said. "Not really."

"Can you show me how to drive standard?" I asked.

"I surely can," he replied.

*****

A few weeks after I bought my car I got a call from a friend of mine, high up at Miramax. Let's call him Tino. He's tall, lean, handsome, vaguely Mediterranean-looking, and a great guy, really one of the good guys. He has a summer house up north on Monterey Bay in a small town called Moss Landing and he was inviting a few of his friends up for a week.

I almost turned it down, because being stuck in the same house with a bunch of people I didn't really know didn't sound too appealing. But I did end up accepting. My family had a cottage on Lake Muskoka when I was a kid and I could remember it so vividly; the docks, the chairs, the lake (so cold and pure). Fishing and waterskiing and all of that stuff. Maybe it was just what the doctor ordered, and anyway, I could drive up in my new car.

So I said yes.

The day before I was scheduled to leave, Tino called again and asked if I could possibly drive up another one of his friends. I said of course, before I found out who he meant. Then he told me, and inside I cringed, because he said the name of a very famous, very beautiful actress with whom I had an odd kind of history.

If I were to tell you this actress's name, there's no doubt you'd recognize it. Even my mom would get this one, I think. But I'm not really sure I'd like to drag her into this, since she values her privacy and it's too early to say how things are going to turn out between us. So let's just call her "Hersh."

Anyway, I'd met Hersh a few years earlier, shortly after the *Star Wars* book had come out. I don't normally have much luck with girls but I got along with Hersh famously. I wasn't nervous to talk to her because I figured I had no chance and we had a great conversation about politics and philosophy because I was curious about whether she was really as smart as everyone said. We kept in touch, off and on. Obviously she was very busy.

The last time we'd spoken was before *Half-Life* came out. I got a little drunk and told her that my writing had been genius, that I'd had to fight the suits tooth and nail but I'd gotten my vision. And Hersh, who is a nice girl but can be a little snotty at times, put up her nose a little bit and made some sort of dismissive comment about how it was a bit rich to talk about vision when I'd adapted a video game. Now that got my back up and I told her that my screenplay was art, it was great art, and that I was going to get nominated for an Oscar. And she snorted at this and said it wasn't likely. And so on, back and forth, until somehow I managed to extract a promise that she would make out with me if I got nominated for an Oscar.

Well. As you may know, *Half-Life* shattered box office records and had a stellar ranking of 97% on Rotten Tomatoes and the studio hyped the shit out of it going into the awards season and, well, I guess it was a slow year for movies based on classic works of literature or something because I snuck in there somehow. But I never called Hersh to collect, or even to make a joke about it and let her off the hook. All of a sudden it was weird for me, and even though I saw her at the Academy Awards, I didn't even walk over to say hi.

So I guess I'd kind of been ignoring her (although she hadn't called me either) and I hadn't collected on my bet. Now what was I supposed to say when I picked her up? I had to say something. It was stressing me out when the whole point of this trip was to help me relax. But there wasn't really anything to do, so I picked up the phone and gave her a call.

She didn't answer so I left a message and went back to work. After ten minutes she called me back.

"Hi Charlie," she said.

"Hello Hersh. How are you doing?"

"I'm fine."

"Well, that's good. It's been a while."

"So are you going to this thing tomorrow?"

"Yeah," I said. "I'm driving up. I can pick you up whenever."

"I was thinking of going later. I have a lot of things to take care of and that way we'd miss traffic."

"Fine," I said.

"Is eight all right?"

"Eight's fine. What's your address?"

She gave me the name of an expensive condominium building near the ocean.

"Okay," I said, "Just one more thing. I have a pretty small car, so I'm not sure how much stuff you can bring."

"What's that supposed to mean?"

"Nothing, just that I don't have a lot of trunk space."

"Well, how much is too much?" she asked.

"I don't know, it's just, space is limited, that's all."

"Well," she said, "I'll keep that in mind."

"Okay," I said, feeling like a jackass. "I'll see you tomorrow."

"Okay," she said, and hung up.

The next day I headed out in my new car. I had barely driven it since I bought it and I was rather glad the streets of L.A. were, if not exactly deserted, at least quieter than normal. I stalled the car once at a busy intersection and the douchebag behind me was quick on the horn. Other than that I arrived without incident and parked out front and called up to Hersh on my phone.

She came down with the doorman and five suitcases. When she saw the car she stopped and lowered her glasses and said: "You've got to be kidding me."

I got out of the car and looked at her bags. The GT's tiny trunk was practically full with my one duffel bag.

"Five bags? I told you I had a small car."

"I thought you meant the Prius," she said. "What the hell is this?"

"Uh," I said. "It's a GT."

"When did you get this?"

"Last week."

"I didn't even know you liked cars."

"I don't."

"Are you having a midlife crisis or something?"

I didn't answer; I suddenly felt as if I might cry.

She looked at me, with her expensive sunglasses and coat and shirt and pants and shoes, the five bags around her, the doorman waiting respectfully in the background. I looked at my shoes and thought, don't cry, Jesus, you fucking pussy, do not cry.

Hersh pursed her mouth a little bit and then shook her head.

"Well, will it all fit?"

"I don't know," I said.

It did all fit. We jammed a couple of the smaller ones in the trunk and put the rest in the back seat. Hersh had to put her seat all the way forward but she was a very small woman, just a few inches over five feet, and that wasn't much of a problem.

"All right," I said, "I just learned to drive standard, so bear with me."

"What happened to the Prius?"

"Where did you get this idea that I had a Prius?"

"You had a Prius before, I thought."

"That was one of Josh's cars," I said.

Josh Hartnett had starred as Gordon Freeman in the *Half-Life* movie and I'd lived at his house for about a year. I think he'd bought the Prius when he was trying to bang this Danish model who was very concerned about global warming. I drove it because I was too scared to drive any of his expensive cars.

"How did you even know I drove a Prius?"

"Amy told me," she said. "Amy said you didn't believe in luxury cars and that you liked driving a Hybrid because it was quiet and good for the environment."

'Amy' is what I'll call my ex-girlfriend; the one who broke my heart.

I gritted my teeth a bit and pulled out onto the road.

"Well," I said, "people change, I guess."

We drove in silence for a while and then Hersh took out her phone.

"Do you mind if I make some calls?"

"Go ahead," I said.

Say what you will about my decision to betray my environmental principles, the GT was fun to drive. It leapt forward when you pressed down on the gas and it was glued to the road around the corners. I was nervous on stick shift; there was always the chance of me messing up and going into fourth when I meant sixth, or something. But it made things interesting, and I managed to avoid doing anything stupid.

Hersh hung up her phone and curled up her legs underneath her and leaned up against the window. I could see that she was looking at me out of the corner of my eye. I didn't say anything.

"How much did the car cost?" she finally asked.

"A lot," I said.

"Was it just a whim?"

"Yes."

"I guess you're rich now," she said.

"I can't complain."

"Have you bought anything else?"

"Not really. I bought a house in Malibu."

"I know."

I didn't ask how. "I helped my sister and my brother-in-law buy a house, and paid my parents' mortgage," I said. "Then I gave some money to charity. The rest of it just sort of piled up. I don't know what to do with it."

"So you bought a car."

"This car is a limited edition," I said.

"Mmm," she said.

"Anyway, like you don't buy anything stupid," I said. "How much did your sunglasses cost?"

"My friend gave them to me," she said.

"Well," I said, "I'm sure you spend money stupidly on some things. I bet your underwear cost like two hundred bucks or something."

"Don't ask me about my underwear."

"Okay, fine. My point is, after you get a certain amount of money, there's nothing left to spend it on that isn't stupid. The basics only cost so much, and you can't sensibly invest it all, or give it all charity. Not all of it."

"How do you know?"

"Fine," I said. "I guess I don't know."

"So why'd you buy the car?" she asked.

"I don't know Hersh. I'm just feeling a bit down."

"You don't have anything to feel down about."

"I know that. It doesn't make it any easier."

"I don't get it," she said, contemptuously, or so it seemed to me.

"Yeah, of course you don't," I shot back, nettled. "You've been famous since you were what, thirteen? Then you go off to Harvard and win awards and everyone loves you. I bet you never sat around wondering about the point of it all."

"No, not really," she said. "What's the point of that?"

"There is no point, I'm not saying there's a point. I'm saying for the rest of us, for us ordinary mortals, we sometimes don't always know what we want and just go out and get it. Okay? Sometimes we don't know what we want so we go buy some fucking car or something out of desperation."

"All right, calm down, all right? I'm sorry."

She smoothed her skirt down a little. "I'm sorry, I'm too bossy. You can feel depressed and buy a car if you want. I'm not your mom."

"No, I'm sorry Hersh," I said. "I didn't mean it."

"It's all right," she said. "I don't mean to be disapproving. I just wanted to ask a question."

I flexed my fingers on the wheel. I pretended like I didn't know what was happening to me, but of course I did. I had gotten the things I had thought I wanted most in the world and they hadn't made me happy and so I was in the process of losing all hope.

"It's just I got everything I want in life and I'm still unhappy," I said, "and I ... I just feel down. That's all."

"It's perfectly natural," Hersh said. "That's basic psychology."

We were off the main highway, now on a little two lane road running near the ocean. Ahead of us was a truck labelled "Joe's Ice Company."

"Look at that truck," I said. "Think about Joe, there. Starting his own company. Do you know how much work it is to start your own company? It never ends. And it's not glamorous. Driving ice around is not a glamorous job. No one likes ice. I bet Joe started out driving an ice truck, but while his buddies were getting drunk every night, Joe stayed up late learning about the ice business and saved his money till he could start his own. Then he probably worked like a dog for years to get it off the ground. His wife probably had to be the bookkeeper, even when she was trying to raise the kids. Finally he started hiring employees, he built up clients, now he sits on the dock, up at fucking Moss Landing for all I know, and lives the sweet life."

She sat there looking at me prettily, silently making it clear that she presumed this was going somewhere.

"And did Joe ever sit around and wonder: am I really into ice? Am I really passionate about ice? Is this what I really want to do? Am I making a difference? Should I go back to school? No. Joe didn't think those things. Joe just went full bore on ice, which is stupid. No one cares about ice. Anyone can just make it themselves in their freezer. But now

Joe has something he can look back on, something real, that he accomplished."

I tensed up. I could feel it all through my shoulders and back.

"I just ... I don't know why I'm not like that. I don't know why I always have to wonder about everything."

"You've accomplished a lot of things," Hersh said.

I shifted up a gear and blew past the ice truck. Hersh craned her head and watched it for a moment.

We'd been driving for a while and it was night. To our left was the ocean, dark and unimaginably vast. The headlights illuminated a short pool in front of us. The road curved left and right.

"Well, it's nice to talk to you," Hersh said. "It's been a while."

"Yeah."

"I didn't know if you were angry at me or something."

"I wasn't angry."

"Was it the bet?" she asked.

I was quiet for a moment, and then I said: "Yeah, I guess it was the bet."

She didn't reply. We drove in silence.

Once I opened my mouth but I just closed it again.

She shifted a little in her seat.

"I'm sorry about that," I said. "It's just, you know, we made the bet, and then I got nominated, and it really changed a lot of things for me. Or I thought it did, at the time."

"You didn't think you'd get nominated," she said.

"No, I did," I said. "I mean, it's stupid, but I really did. Just like I said when the book would be a bestseller and everyone said I was crazy. I really felt good about *Half-Life*. And then I was looking forward to it. I really thought, you know, it might have changed things. With us. I mean. And then, when it happened, I just felt. I don't know. Afraid, or empty inside, or something. Like there wasn't anything to say."

"I see," Hersh said.

I looked over at her and she looked a little pissed. Her mouth was set and her head was turned away from me a little. She was looking out the window.

"But, I hope you're not mad at me. Are you?"

Hersh said, no.

"I'm worried you're mad. It's not you, it's me, I'm just all tied up in knots. I didn't mean to seem angry at you."

Hersh looked at me, with something that I interpreted as scorn, and then looked away again. I looked at the road. For the life of me, I couldn't think of a thing to say. We drove the rest of the way in complete silence.

Moss Landing isn't even really a town. There's a natural bay that juts in a little bit at the mouth of a river with houses and docks around at irregular intervals. Miles of beach to the south and north.

Tino had a sprawling home on the inside of the bay, up among some tall trees. It wasn't on a beach like some of the other properties. It was more like the cottages I remembered from Lake Muskoka, with a boathouse jutting out over the water. We came up and I parked the car, pleased that I hadn't killed us both.

"Well," I said, "here we are."

Hersh turned her head and looked at me. I thought she looked really pissed.

"What is it, Hersh?" I said. "I don't get it. I'm sorry, I was just awkward. It's not that I didn't like you, I'm just shy or stupid or something. Okay? Don't be mad."

"You didn't have to get nominated for an Academy Award," Hersh said.

"What?" I said.

"The bet," Hersh said. "You're really stupid. Do you know that?"

"Don't call me stupid," I said.

"Do you think the bet meant anything?" Hersh said. "Why ... I just can't believe it. Do you think there's some kind of magic trick to things? Do you think it meant anything to me? Anything at all?"

"I'm sorry," I said. And boy did I mean it. "It's just tough for me."

"What? What's tough for you? What are you talking about?"

"Look, I don't know, this stuff."

She turned away and opened the car door.

"You could have called me!" I said.

She shut the door and walked up to the house by herself, not before making a sound that might have been a sob. I wondered whether I was supposed to carry her bags for her. I put my head on the steering wheel and cursed myself. I felt like King Midas in reverse.

*****

Inside everyone was relaxing with a few drinks. I told Tino I was thinking of doing a little writing so he put me in the boathouse.   I had a nice, clean, empty room up above the boats and a desk where I could set up my computer and my books. I told them I was coming right back but I took a moment instead to sit down and think.

I was thinking about Hersh, of course, and what she'd said, but I didn't know what to do, or even what I wanted. I tried to write for a bit to settle myself down; I had to finish an Aquaman comic for next Thursday. But I couldn't do that either. I just wanted it to be over, only I didn't know what 'it' was. I wanted to get up and leave everything but there wasn't anywhere else to go.

I didn't go back to the house for drinks; I just lay in bed, unable to sleep, for a very long time.

The next morning Tino woke me up by knocking on my door.

"Did something happen between you and Hersh?"

"Yeah," I said.

Shock was written all over his face.

"Is there something going on between you two?"

"No," I said, "I mean, I don't know."

"Holy shit!" he exclaimed.

"Don't tell anyone."

"Don't worry man," he said. People always say that before they tell everyone. "So what are you going to do?"

"I don't know," I said.

"I'm having the neighbours over for a barbeque," he said. "You should come out to that."

And so, after spending the morning listlessly working on an adaptation of *The Confessions of Nat Turner* that was never going to get made, I did.

The house was a little ways away from the bay, separated from the boathouse by a long green stretch of long grass and wildflowers. There were a ton of people milling around, a lot of who worked in the movies. I did a lot of grinning and handshaking and struggling to remember people's names. I could see Hersh sitting in the sun on a white plastic recliner, talking to somebody's wife. Eventually someone brought her a vegetarian hot dog. She never looked at me. I kept looking at her, again and again, like a kicked dog.

Eventually I fell in with one of the neighbour's kids. He was a tall, blond, athletic-looking boy named Ty and he and his friends seemed to have sprung out of a back-to-school catalogue. They all wore pastel golf shirts with popped collars and they had spotless white teeth and spiky, jelled hair. But I get along pretty well with that type; it's not a hard type to get along with if you set your ego aside.

Pretty soon I was telling them stories about filming *Half-Life* and they were telling me stories about how drunk they'd gotten at this frat party at UCLA and we were all debating about who was the pound-for-pound king in the

UFC. I flicked one glance over at Hersh during this time and saw that she was looking at me. I felt like I'd scored a point, somehow.

I drank a few beers and when Ty invited us all to go for a ride on his boat, I said yes.

We walked across to his house and down to his boathouse. The boat was one of those streamlined white monstrosities, nothing but forward momentum. There were seven of us, five men and two women. Ty jumped on the gas and we blasted out into the bay.

Moss Landing was built around a small bay that jutted deeper inland from the broader Mandalay Bay. The water was a deep, almost unnatural blue, very unlike the black lakes of my youth. There wasn't a cloud in the sky. I was leaning back in the soft cushion of my chair, feeling good about myself as the boat skipped over the waves. I looked at one of the girls, she couldn't have been more than twenty one, and tipped her a wink. She smiled; I thought her orthodontist must have been very proud.

Ty turned back towards land a little bit and we started passing by other houses on the water, about five hundred metres or so from the shore. Suddenly some of his friends started pointing excitedly and Ty turned the boat.

"What are we doing?" I said, but I was largely drowned out by the roaring motor. Then I saw him:

A man floating in an inner tube had drifted out into the water, say about a hundred yards from the shore. He was fat and middle-aged and orange with the sun. There was a can of beer winking in his hand and he looked completely at peace with the world.

All of a sudden I felt a wave of compassion for this man. He wasn't fit enough to be from Hollywood. I thought he must be some small business person who had made his fortune in mail-order motorcycle parts or contracting or something. His whole life, I imagined, he'd worked like a dog and he'd bought a beautiful house up in Moss Landing and now he was trying to catch some rays lying on an inner tube, but his neighbour's douchebag kids were about to ruin it for him.

All of a sudden I knew who he was; he was Joe, of Joe's Ice Company.

But there was nothing I could do. We blew past Joe going a hundred miles an hour. The tube flipped over and Joe disappeared into the sea. Everyone on the boat was roaring with laughter and they started high-fiving each other as Ty turned the boat back out towards the centre of the bay.

"Fuck this," I said.

Suddenly I was sick with myself. This was who I had become, I thought. A douchebag. I was rich and successful and I was a douche. Here I was, jetting around on my friend's boat, depressed, too much of a sissy to go hit on a movie star that liked me. I hated my life.

The girl was looking at me, a little concerned.

"Are you all right?" she said.

"I'm going to swim back," I said.

"What?" she said.

I put my foot on the side of the boat and jumped.

The first shock was the temperature; the second was the salt. Swimming in a lake feels so clean and pure. The ocean was freezing brine. I couldn't see a foot in front of me under water and when I came back up my eyes were stinging like mad. It was like there was a film clinging to me and my mouth felt like it was full of blood. I spat once.

But I felt good too. For years I'd swum competitively, getting up at five in the morning to do lap after lap in the pool, and then swimming again at night. During the *Half-Life* shoot I'd even trained a little for an Ironman that I'd never done. I could tread water basically indefinitely and I wasn't afraid of drowning at all. I was only a few hundred metres from shore.

The boat rocketed on away from me, then started to slow and turn back. I dived under the water and did a few strokes. I looked down. There was only darkness, with a few ribbons of light cutting down into the murk before fading into nothing. Little bits of things floated before my eyes. I came up into the sun again and took a deep breath.

I was wearing cargo shorts, a tight t-shirt, underwear. I kicked off my flip flops and stuck them in my pockets. Then I started to swim.

"Hey!" Ty was yelling from the boat. "What are you doing?"

"I'm going to swim back," I said.

"What?"

I flipped over onto my back and did a little elementary back stroke.

"I'm going to swim back. Leave me alone."

"Are you retarded?"

"At least I'm not a fucking douchebag," I said. "Turn your collar down, for Christ's sake."

I turned back onto my stomach and put my face in the water and started to swim and wouldn't you know it, those douchebags ditched me there, no lifejacket or anything. I lifted my head and they were burning away, only the girl hanging over the end of the boat to see how I was doing.

I wasn't worried. I felt good. The ocean wasn't what I'd been expecting; instead of being refreshed, I felt like I needed a shower. But it was wonderful to be a million miles away from anything. Almost like flying.

I swam for another ten minutes, during which time I travelled perhaps a hundred metres. It occurred to me that the boat really wasn't coming back and all of a sudden I felt a kind of cold sensation. An inkling of fear. I was pretty tired. My clothes were dragging me down and the waves made swimming in a straight line very difficult.

Had they really left me out here? I wondered. Jesus. If I died, they'd go to jail.

Not that I was going to die. There really wasn't any chance of that. I can tread water for hours. Honestly. If it came down to it, I'd turn onto my back and just coast in slowly.

I swam for another ten minutes and I could have sworn that I was getting further away. Everything on the shore was so small. It was so strange to think that I could die out here (not that I was going to) only about a sixty-second sprint away, on land.

And that's when my mind started to play tricks on me. I'm easily frightened; by noises, by the dark, by sudden movements in the corner of my vision. It's part of being a writer; you have a good imagination, you get good at scaring yourself. And suddenly I could picture all sorts of monsters, lurking, just a few inches below my feet. Ancient scaly beasts, evil and hungry, with sharp fangs or beaks and long tentacles. Monsters, awoken and disturbed by my intrusion into their domain. One moment I'd be swimming along the surface, the next poof! I'd disappear without a trace, without a peep, beneath these cold and poisonous waves.

With no one to mourn me.

I started to speed up my swimming; it made no noticeable difference to how quickly I was approaching the shore. A wave smacked me in the face and I swallowed salt water. Coughing, I slowed and turned my head away, and that's when I saw the dorsal fin of the shark.

My heart stopped in my chest and I immediately sank about a foot beneath the water and opened my eyes. It was rushing at me with unbelievable speed; as fast as a car, faster than a man could run on land. At first it was only a vague blurry shape in the distance, weaving in between the shafts of light, ducking its head side to side like a boxer. Then all of a sudden, it was just there; rolling to the left, exposing that tremendous mouth with the teeth curled inward like fingers, black eyes turning over white.

And it barrelled into me like a bull.

I was screaming under the water. I wish I could express to you how evil it looked, how malevolent. The spiky and inhuman fangs, the dark and gaping jaws, the eyes as dead as marbles. The water was turning red in front of my eyes. I can't remember exactly what happened. I was too frightened. I think I kicked at it and it bit one of my feet and then I kicked at it again. It had me in its mouth and it shook me a bit and its teeth serrated into my calf like a saw. I was screaming and swallowing salt water and kicking and then all of a sudden it was gone.

I couldn't breathe so I burst up through to the surface. I was gasping for air and screaming and weeping. I looked around but I couldn't see that fin anywhere and then it hit me and dragged me under again.

There wasn't any pain at all throughout this, if you can believe me. I swear to god I didn't feel a thing.

Now it was shaking me and tearing up my thigh. Trying to rip a chunk out of me. I curled up to its face and started jabbing it in the eyes with my thumbs, and then punching it in the gills. It was as implacable as a machine. The shark was around six of seven feet long, blue on the top, white underneath. I later identified it as a shortfin mako shark, a species which, according to the International Shark Attack File, has only attacked humans eight times in the past four hundred years. Lucky fucking me.

At this point I think I either passed out or almost passed out. Anyway, for a while I don't have any memories. I just remember being loose again and swimming back up to the surface of water and breathing desperately and then watching the shark swim away from me. Now my legs started to hurt unbearably and I screamed but the wind had picked up and my voice was drowned out and anyway there was no one on the shore. The closest houses to me were closed up and dark.

"Help me!" I screamed up at that indifferent sky. "Oh god, help me please! Help me!"

I started paddling back towards land but I could barely move my legs. It was all I could do to stay afloat. And when I turned over my shoulder to look behind me I saw the shark rushing up on me again.

"No!" I said, then I took a deep breath and went under the water. This time I curled my legs under me and when the shark rushed in I caught its nose with my hands and wrapped my legs around its belly and kept its mouth away from me.

It opened and closed its jaws with a stupid kind of eagerness that reminded me, for some reason, of a dog. And then I had a terrible realization; that this creature, as terrifying and monstrous as it appeared to me, bore me no ill will. It was just a dumb animal, so stupid it didn't even know that sharks weren't supposed to eat human beings. It was only hungry. This was no more an epic battle of good versus evil than a cat eating a mouse. I was just in the wrong place, that was all. Out here I was not special or loved or famous. There were no laws or morals of any kind. I was just a chunk of meat, floating in salt water, and anything that wanted to take a bite of me could.

The shark wrestled with me, and tried to wriggle closer. Suddenly it put on a sudden burst of speed and we actually leapt out of the water, almost a full meter into the air. For an instant, I could smell its rotten breath. It twisted around and tried to get at me and I braced my arm and punched it in the gills again.

When we hit the water the force of the blow knocked me into its mouth and it took a bite of my pectoral muscles, nuzzled there like some kind of demonic infant. I pushed my way free but I was bleeding into its nose and mouth and it seemed to be going into a frenzy.

I started to gray out again, but this time I fought it as hard as I could. I looked into its eye, into its mute fish's eye, and I tried desperately to see something there. I wanted this fish to see me if it was going to kill me. To really see me, to know who I was, to know what it was doing, to give this moment, so important for me, some kind of meaning. But of course there was nothing there.

I don't think I could have lasted another minute, but then something hit us.

The shark and I were jarred apart. I couldn't see anything; it was just a lot of big fishes moving around. I looked for the surface and swam back up for air. I didn't do any screaming when I got there this time, although I was in unbelievable pain. My left calf felt like it was barely attached and there were deep wounds in my right thigh. The wound in my chest felt a little more superficial, but there was no question I was bleeding a lot. I looked up at the sky again and waited for the shark to come back.

But it didn't. I saw it come to the surface again, rear out, showing off all those teeth, but then it fell back and I could see there were other fish there too. At first I thought they were more sharks, but eventually I realized they were dolphins. Two or three of them, rushing up and butting the shark with their heads, like sleek little missiles. They were circling me in a tight group, sometimes looking at me eye to eye, lifting their faces out of the water and chattering, but mostly keeping their heads down and swimming fast.

The shark was gone. Its fin cut through the waves as it swam out to sea, quickly, leaving me behind.

"Help," I said.

I started to cry, just like a little girl.

"Please help me," I said, and reached out for them.

I suppose I had visions of one of them carrying me to shore, but they were already leaving.

"Fuck," I said, "fuck no, don't leave me!"

They slipped away, one by one. The last one fired a shot of water out of his blowhole. A few moments later I saw them jumping, closer to shore.

"No!" I screamed, "no!"

And then something funny happened again, because I don't remember anything for a while, and when I start remembering them again everything was sepia, and I could barely hear.

It was all I could do to keep my head above the water. I knew I was going to die and a curious sense of peace spread through me. It was all right. I didn't feel separate from things any more. I didn't feel like a stranger in the ocean, like an intruder. I felt like I'd finally come home. It was no exaggeration to say I felt better in those moments, floating in the ocean and bleeding, than I'd ever done in my new mansion in Malibu.

But then the boat came to rescue me and ruined everything.

At the sound of the motor something woke in me and I started to swim, even through the pain, my legs barely moving. I was weeping every time I lifted my face to take a breath.

The speed boat was racing towards me. On board were Ty and Hersh. They saw me when I lifted my arm and jetted up close and cut the engine about fifteen feet away and that's when I started to scream.

"Help! Help me! Hurry! Please!"

Ty started to smile at me. Hersh looked a little embarrassed.

"It's all right, Charlie," she said.

I was bawling like an infant when they came up for me. I lifted my hand and Ty took it and pulled. When he saw the bite in my chest he was so surprised he let me go, and I plunged under the water.

And I tell you, I swear to god, I almost did not come back up. I must have fallen three or four feet below the surface and it seemed like too much, just too much, to find the strength to swim back up again. But somehow I did.

When I came back up, the expression on Ty's face said that he knew he was in a fuckload of trouble. Hersh was just screaming and screaming, her eyes starting out of her head, her hands pressed against her cheeks. Ty grabbed me by the back of my shirt and hauled me out of the ocean. When they saw my legs, and all the blood cascading down into the water, Ty's shoulders heaved like he was going to throw up. Hersh fell totally silent and dug her fingers into the side of her face.

"It's okay man," Ty said, "hey, it's okay."

I started to laugh.

They laid me down on the white leather seats of the boat and I bled everywhere. I was laughing like mad. Hersh pressed her little hands down on the wounds on my leg and got blood on her too. Ty was driving the boat like a lunatic and now he was sobbing, "Oh god, oh man, oh my god."

I was laughing and laughing. The cords on my neck were standing out. I couldn't breathe. Blood spurted everywhere. I looked at the sky for a while and then my eyes rolled back. I laughed and laughed.

*****

The doctors assured me that it really wasn't all that bad. I was very lucky, in fact, the shark had missed the aorta when it bit my thigh. They reattached my calf to the bone, stitched up my front, watched me for a few days. Then they sent me back to Monterey Bay to finish my vacation.

You may have read in the tabloids or on TMZ or elsewhere that I got in trouble for punching a doctor during my stay, which is true. The doctor in question urged me, when I was fully healed, to "not be afraid to get back in there."

Tino and I shared a bottle of nice Islay Scotch whisky. He said everyone in Hollywood was asking about me. I told him the whole story and he laughed like crazy. For some reason the story was funny when I told it. He said I should write it down. I told him to fuck that. Eventually I passed out in his Laz-E-Boy.

I dreamed of the shark that night. It wasn't a nightmare. I just dreamed of it out there, swimming in the deep, endless and uniform blue, no higher purpose than to wander.

When I woke up there was a blanket on me and it was after noon. I hobbled back to the boathouse and I saw Hersh on the dock. She was wearing a little yellow sundress and sunglasses and a hat and reading *Gravity's Rainbow*. There was a glass of Pimm's on the table next to her. She put the book down when I came over.

"Hi there," I said.

"Hi," she said.

"Can I join you?"

She shrugged.

I sat down on the chair across from her.

"Thank you," I said, "for saving my life."

She shrugged and looked away.

"Ty told me you made him go back."

"Well somebody had to," she said. "I can't believe he just left you there."

"Well, I told him to."

"Well, you're an idiot," she said.

"I guess," I said.

She picked up her book.

"Why didn't you come visit me?" I said.

She didn't say anything. Then she shrugged a bit.

"I missed you. I was in the hospital. Why didn't you come to say hi? Even for ten minutes?"

She put her book down and then she looked at me and she shouted: "Why would you do that? Why would you jump out of a boat in the middle of the ocean? What's wrong with you? You have a perfectly nice life."

"I know," I said.

"Why would you try to kill yourself like that?"

"I didn't try to kill myself."

She paused, and I saw by the way that her shoulders moved that she was crying a little, and my heart was touched.

"Hersh, I didn't try to kill myself, I was just annoyed with those douchebags and I wanted to go swimming."

"Why'd you take such a risk?" her voice quavering.

"It wasn't a risk."

"You got attacked by a shark, you idiot."

"I forgot, Hersh, okay, I admit, I admit I forgot about the sharks. Okay? I forgot about them. There are no sharks in Canada."

"Well you still could have drowned," she said.

She reached under her glasses and wiped her eyes.

"No," I said, "I'm a very good swimmer."

"Still, you didn't have a life jacket."

"I'm a good swimmer! I was on the swim team. I can tread water basically forever."

"No one can tread water forever."

"Anyone can," I said. "You can. I could teach you in five minutes."

"Whatever," she said.

"Get your swimsuit," I said. "I can show you in five minutes."

She looked at me and pursed her lips a little and then she took off her hat and sunglasses and stood up and undid her dress and it dropped down around her feet. There she was in the sun, next to the glinting ocean, naked except for her bra and sensible panties, a beautiful woman in her mid thirties. A famous actress, but without lighting and makeup and airbrush and posing and multiple takes she didn't seem any different from Amy or the other women I'd dated, just a good looking woman, a little short, that's all.

She pinched her nose and jumped in the water and came up gasping for air and paddling like a dog.

"Stop that," I said.

I hobbled over a bit and then lay down on my stomach and scooted over to the edge of the dock. Hersh was only a few feet away for me. She was panting.

"Stop," I said, "you look and sound like a dog."

"Well, I'm going to sink," she said.

I reached out and caught her shoulder with one hand and said: "Stop struggling. Just float."

"I'll sink!"

"I've got you, you're not going to sink. Stop struggling."

She stopped and I grabbed her other shoulder with my other hand and kept her above the water.

"Okay," I said, "now only use your hands. Just wave them back and forth right under the surface of the water."

She started doing it.

"Now I'm going to let you go."

"Okay," she said.

I let her go and she started to speed up.

"Slow down," I said.

"I can't!"

"Yes you can," I said. "Go as slow as you can and still keep your head above water."

She slowed down a bit, and then a bit more.

"You'll tire yourself out. Go as slow as you can. Slow, big movements."

She slowed down some more, so that her head was just above the waves, like a cork.

"You see?" I said. "You see how easy that is? You're not even using your legs."

She looked at me with her bright little eyes and just floated.

"That's the trick," I said. "The trick is not to work too hard. You'll tire yourself out if you work too hard, and you'll sink. The trick is to just float, to let everything else to the work. Do as little as possible."

She moved her hands back and forth, back and forth. And then I had what can only be described as a hallucination, or a vivid imagination. I saw the shark rising up from beneath her, from the deep, its jaws open, its eyes empty and hungry. The fear I felt must have shown on my face because she followed my gaze, alarmed, and started to struggle again.

"It's nothing," I said, "I just got scared. Take my hand."

I pulled her out quickly. She came up all wet in my arms.

"Let me go," she said.

But I held her there for a moment, no matter what she said.

Because here is the secret: There was not really any difference between the sharks and the dolphins, they just followed their programming blindly, whether it was to save or feed. There is nothing special or wonderful about this world or anything in it. It is all indifferent to us and our concerns, neither hostile nor helpful, but merely unfolding at its own good pace. Just a lot of stuff that happens.

If I was waiting for meaning, for magic, I would wait forever in vain. Everything would roll on by, serenely, uncaring. The only things troubled with me mysterious creatures of deep. That the forces that could save or destroy could be so indifferent was what was so shocking. I didn't want to be like them. Just a thing. I wanted to really see.

"Charlie," she said, squirming a little, "let me go."

"I don't want to, Hersh," I said. "I don't want to."

On the average, only those prisoners could keep alive who, after years of trekking from camp to camp, had lost all scruples in their fight for existence; they were prepared to use every means, honest and otherwise, even brutal force, theft, and betrayal of their friends, in order to save themselves. We who have come back, by aid of many lucky chances or miracles – we know: the best of us did not return.

Viktor E. Frankl – *Man's Search for Meaning*

3 Nothing to Worry About

When we arrived at the house, we did the same sort of thing we'd done at the diner. I rang the bell to the front door while Wilder circled around to the back. A very old man opened the door and listened to my rambling story with compassionate eyes until he heard his wife start screaming.

Afterwards Wilder sat in front of the television eating ice cream out of the tub while I prowled around the house. I went upstairs to the bathroom and ran the warm water over my thin, cold hands to scrub the blood from underneath my fingers and then I looked up. It hadn't been long since I'd seen my image reflected in the counter at the diner, but I found myself startled all over again.

If you asked me to describe myself, I'd tell you I was about average height, but very broad in the chest, and in pretty good shape from all those jiu-jitsu classes and the trips to the gym. I'd say I had short black hair that I parted to the side and locked into a place with a judicious amount of gel that I applied with a plastic comb. I'd tell you I was a dentist with a successful practice in Oakville and a tie rack in my closet and that I had a wife who I love very much (no children yet though).

How hard to reconcile all this (Oakville, my wife, our non-children, the tie rack) with the dreadful figure that peered at me through the mirror? So thin that his bones jut through his skin like jagged rocks poking above the surface of the sea. His hair shorn short and his beard long. Thin neck and wrists rattling around in the filthy rags that hang on him like a blanket cast over a corpse. And the eyes. The only part of him that looks alive. Wet and shining, as if someone had hung a lamp behind them.

And I couldn't deny that I'd changed inside too, and that the changes inside were even more drastic than the ones you could see. That's why I started to write this. It's not that I want to make excuses for the things I did. I made the choices I made, and I could have chosen otherwise. It's just that I want to let this person out, the person inside me, underneath all this. I just want him to be seen.

*****

My father was a dentist who hated being a dentist. He thought it was boring. He wasn't particularly good with people and married one of his hygienists, a religious Filipino woman fifteen years his junior. I defied his wishes by following him into the profession and my mother into the church. He preferred my sister, who earned one fine arts degree after another and, the day of my arrest, was living in my basement and working on a novel.

One characteristic my father and I did share was an overwhelming, self-destructive honesty. We could both be a little blunt at times, if not outright rude. The key difference between us, in this respect, was that I had some circumspection, whereas he did not. So, once the new political arrangement solidified, after the initial trials and travails, we were both probably going to get into trouble, but he was going to get into trouble first.

My father wasn't a rebel or anything like that. He certainly wasn't a member of the organized underground. As far as I know, there wasn't ever any organized underground, for all the people that were convicted for belonging to it. He just didn't have any sense, my dad. And it was an era that required a certain level of tact.

There was this continuous air of political sensitivity hung in the air. A feeling that any conversation on any topic at all could suddenly turn dangerous. Even if you said something like, say, this sidewalk is in rough shape. Well, what did that say about your opinion of our government? Were you implying it couldn't take care of sidewalks? Were you criticizing our leaders? In this time of crisis? You see.

I got the call at the office while I was poking one of my patients in the gums. My receptionist said it was an emergency so I left the poor guy in the chair with the light shining in his eyes and tubes snaking out of his mouth.

My mother was in tears over the phone. She told me they'd arrested my father and asked me if there wasn't someone I could call.

My father would have laughed at her. *Someone to call?* he'd have said: *Someone to call? Like who? The police? The politicians? The press? The army? Hey, guess what? They're the ones doing this to us! There's no one to call. No one at all.*

As I said, I have a lot more tact than my father, but no less honesty. I simply told my mother no, there wasn't anybody we could call.

*****

The police came to me and asked me a lot of questions about my father. This put me in a difficult position. If I said I had suspicions about him, then why didn't I denounce him myself? And if I didn't suspect him, well then, why not? Because no one is arrested by mistake. Eventually the arrested person confesses (as they always do) to being a

57

highly-ranked member of the opposition and his friends and family fall under suspicion due to their association with an admitted traitor to the regime. That's if the arrested person doesn't implicate them directly in their confession, something which will depend strictly on the whims of whoever drafted it.

I refused again and again to say anything bad about my father. The police (both uniformed and secret) that spoke to me in a series of "voluntary" interviews seemed keen just to have me denounce him. They never came out and said so. They just pushed his confession in front of me and asked me to admit that it must be true, that the proof was right there.

I remember the last conversation I had with the Party official in charge of my father's case. We were sitting in his Toronto office in a squat concrete building at Sheppard and Yonge. He was waving my father's confession in one hand and talking and talking. I don't remember what he said. These people yammered on, it was the tone of voice that mattered more than the substance of what they said.

I do remember how he finished though. He said: "I understand you didn't know, but the confession is here, right? You acknowledge that your father confessed to these crimes, right?"

And I looked at him for a long time, and then I just smiled, a little helplessly. Then I got up.

"Don't go, we're not finished."

I walked out. It was a *voluntary* meeting after all.

*****

The next day a group of youth Party members showed up at my office and started screaming at everyone. The patients in the waiting room scattered. My files were overturned, computers stolen. The kid in the chair, just a fifteen year old girl, was marched outside with my staff and me. They put dunce caps on our heads and made us wear sandwich boards with political slogans on them and marched us up and down the street. The women cried the whole time. I just stared at my feet. I didn't feel any kind of shock or disbelief. I was acutely aware of what was happening to me. I almost enjoyed it.

You see, I could tell the kind of people that were going to thrive and survive in this environment. The real oppression was just starting, but it was already clear how things were going to go. No one was going to survive if they didn't lie, cower, whimper, beg, denounce their neighbours. In this brave new world, getting this kind of treatment was almost a feather in your cap. Or so I thought, at the time.

I went back to the office, alone, after they let us go. It was in ruins. I went home and stayed inside with the drapes drawn until the police came to arrest me in the middle of the night two days later.

*****

I was sent to the Don Jail after my arrest. The Don had been overcrowded for years, so much so that it had been criticized by international human rights organizations. Now that it wasn't just full of the usual skids but also loads of regular people (and, I suppose, that there were no more international human rights organizations to complain) the place was rammed. Men slept two to a bed in the bunks, if they got a bed at all. The toilets were backed up and broken. I never, in the four weeks I was there, saw a working shower. Rations were two bologna sandwiches a day, which were basically inedible.

The normal prisoners, the skids, the kind of people who would have been in jail no matter what the regime, despised the political prisoners. In their view, they were straight or righteous cons, while we were fish or queens or bitches. They hated us for our weakness, I think, and there's no denying the political prisoners were pathetic. We'd had no experience being in jail. Even after we became the majority of the population, it was always clear we didn't belong. The skids could smell the fear on us, they could see how green we were, how we didn't know how anything worked. Something about it drove them wild with contempt and rage.

The guard dropped me off in the general prisoner's area, a huge room dominated by long dining tables and plastic benches, absolutely overflowing with people. Within thirty seconds I was approached by three men, all middle-aged, who spread out and surrounded me. They were of indeterminate race (American Indian? Hispanic? Greek?) with long greasy dark hair and faces pitted and eroded by time and substance abuse.

Their leader asked me for my shoes and I told him he couldn't have them.

I was terribly afraid. I felt just awful inside, like I was going to be sick. But there was another feeling in me, a feeling that what was happening was terribly, terribly wrong. And I just couldn't do it. I just couldn't bear to bend over, take off my shoes, and meekly hand them over.

The skid leader stepped forward menacingly and I tried to push past him and he caught me. I tried to pull away but he held my shirt and pushed me back. The other two closed in behind me and so I executed what is called in Brazilian jiu-jitsu a "flying arm-bar." That is, I "pulled guard" (by wrapping my legs around the skid's waist and pulling him down so he was lying on top of me) and took hold of the skid's left arm. Then I lifted my left leg up and rotated my body so I had the skid's elbow resting against my groin and my left leg across the skid's face.

We fell down to the ground and I pulled back on the skid's wrist while pushing forward with my hips and the elbow snapped very easily. I'd never done anything before like that in my life, although I'd practiced the move dozens of time. I was surprised how easily the arm broke.

He started to scream horribly of course and I pushed him away as the other two leapt on me. One of them lay on my side and I got back into guard by wrapping my legs around him and pulling him close.

The other produced a knife from somewhere and started stabbing at me wildly. He was going for my face and so I hid behind the one I was holding on top of me. The blade was hitting the side of my forehead and just butting up against my skull. The noise of everyone shouting was like a physical thing, like a shockwave moving through the air. I was terrified I was going to die.

Eventually the stabbing stopped and I was ripped apart from the skid I was hugging. There were guards everywhere. Their batons whistled through the air and stung like fuck as they cut into flesh. They basically beat the shit out of us. Curling up into a ball, yielding, only seemed to encourage them. The cuts on the side of my head were bleeding heavily and I was smearing my blood all over the linoleum floor. Eventually it stopped and my attackers and I were cuffed and hauled out of the general population.

*****

After the fight they took me to the infirmary to get stitched up and some antibiotics. Then they took me, bleeding and frightened and concussed, into an interrogation room with green tiles on the wall and a broken ceiling fan and harsh fluorescent lighting and no windows. I was interrogated for eight hours after which they switched interrogators and then interrogated me for another eight hours. I was then given a plate of gruel and sent back to my cell where I was not allowed to sleep because a guard watched me from through the bars and hit me with his baton whenever I dozed off.

I didn't get the beatings you heard about other people getting. I wonder if those stories were true. There didn't seem much need to beat anyone up, because I'm not sure how anyone could possibly have stood anything more than what I ended up absorbing. It so thoroughly breaks you to not be able to sleep, to be screamed at and bullied for weeks on end. Even if you stay true to yourself, you don't cry or beg or get scared, you inevitably become filled with a terrible sense of your own powerless to stop this absurd circus from going on. You just start to doubt the essential justice of the universe. If someone had hooked my balls up to a car battery, I might have signed something a little quicker. But I also probably would have gotten my nerve back and recanted afterwards. The way things turned out, although I wasn't precisely spiritless, I certainly never bothered to stand up to the official process any longer. They convinced me that they'd wait me out, no matter how long it took. That's why you lose hope.

Towards the end I was seeing things, little pinwheels of light, shimmering waves of heat or gas, dancing shadows in the corners of my vision. I spoke to people who weren't there. For a moment I might be blind, for another deaf. Sleep was waiting to strike and could steal in at any moment, but the guards were quick to pull me back from the deep.

The day I confessed they brought in a pathetic old man who they claimed was my father. The old man was dreadfully thin and his face had been rearranged (I assume from beatings) and he made a whistling noise when he breathed. He didn't look me in the eye and I couldn't tell if he was my father – everything was shifting around in my vision.

They told me that he was my father and that they would not execute him if I confessed. I looked at my interrogator and I told him, without hesitating, that I would not confess to crimes I had not committed, and that I could not control what they did to my father. I told them his fate was entirely their responsibility. I told them I refused their pathetic attempts to make me in any way complicit in their crimes against the human race.

They took the old man away and a few hours later they told me he had been shot. I don't know if they shot him or not. A few hours later I signed the confession. A rookie interrogator, who didn't know what he was doing, kept shuffling through his notes. I watched him and I realized that it was never going to be over. I told him to give me the confession and I signed. He could not believe his good luck, his face shone. I didn't feel anything. I didn't feel any sense of defeat until much later. At the time, I felt nothing at all, not even a desire to sleep.

*****

The prosecutor made an impassioned speech about my crimes. They sounded very unfamiliar to me, but I didn't think anything of it, since they were made up anyway. But he kept talking about my cousin Donald, which was odd, because I don't have a cousin Donald. Eventually it became clear that the prosecutor was working from the wrong confession. He had to start over. It was amusing to think that the second set of crimes were just as fictional as the first.

My lawyer didn't once speak to me. When it was time tor his argument, he stood and said my crimes were deathly serious and had been proven beyond a shadow of a doubt. He reminded the court he was only defending me because he had been appointed to do so. Then he sat down.

The judge asked me if I had anything to say. I shook my head. There was a hot feeling stirring in the back of my throat. The judge sentenced me to ten years and the guards took me away.

*****

It was the autumn, probably sometime in October. The leaves left on the trees were brilliant. Cloudless blue sky. A wind that cut through to the bone. I came to Union Station on a bus from the prison. I had been wearing the same clothes for weeks and my white shirt had turned yellow. My belt and shoelaces had been returned to me, along with the rest of my meagre possessions.

Most of the other prisoners on the bus were politicals, but there were a number of straight cons as well. There must have been five or six old school buses in our little convoy. They were trying to empty out the Don because the prisoners were coming in faster and faster all the time.

I looked out the window without one coin of hope in my soul. The buses rumbled down King Street, past all the old red brick warehouses that had been converted into restaurants, shops and luxury apartments. We took Jarvis down to Lakeshore and then took York north through the tunnel under the train tracks. The guards loaded us off and took us into the station and up the stairs to the platform which was already crowded with hundreds of people. Then they started taking off the cuffs that bound our wrists and just shoving us forward into the crowd with everyone else.

The trains that were waiting for us were not passenger trains, but cargo cars, big empty boxes, devoid of seats or any human amenities. We were just stuff now, not people, blind raw matter to be shipped to a refinery or forge and transmuted into a more useful form. Bent and twisted until we fit properly into this brave new world.

There were a lot of people who weren't prisoners and I assume had not been officially sentenced and instead were under the impression they were being relocated. Else why would they all carry their suitcases, so full possessions that were now worse than useless that they could barely shut? Why did they grip their relocation papers so tightly and ask useless questions of the soldiers, like when would they be able to call their loved ones or their lawyers or where the bathrooms were or if they could get a drink from somewhere?

The straight cons moved among them shoving and laughing and sometimes calling out to the soldiers. They formed small evil-looking groups and conferred in murmured tones, occasionally lifting their heads to leer at a pretty girl or a particularly defenceless and well-dressed middle-aged man. I squatted down on my heels among the press of the doomed and looked up at the sky and watched my breath rise as vapour around my head.

It would be so cold, up north.

Something screamed – a whistle, an alarm – and suddenly everyone was moving. I was almost knocked on my face as I tried to stand but we were all wedged so tight there was nowhere to fall. I drifted along with the press of humanity. They hadn't assigned those of us who'd come from the jail specific trains. The regular folks who just thought they were being relocated were looking anxiously at their papers and checking numbers. I just hauled myself up into the first car I came to.

No chairs, no washrooms, no lights, no windows except for a few tight slits up near the ceiling designed to provide both ventilation and illumination. There wasn't even any straw or sawdust on the floor, just some rough black rubber mats with shallow grooves.

I was one of the first on board and I took up a place in the far corner. It took almost an hour but the cattle car was so full that there was barely room to stand. The heat and the stench and the sound of weeping were all overwhelming.

"Excuse me," someone was shouting near the door. "I'm on the wrong train! I'm supposed to be on train number forty eight! I can't find my ..."

There was raucous laughter from some of the straight cons, of which there were a good number in the car. They were in the corner opposite from mine and they were looking at the weakness and dismay surrounding them with expressions of unalloyed glee.

The door slid shut with a tremendous clang of rusted metal and plunged us into darkness. A number of people screamed. Outside the whistle howled again, once, twice. A sound to signify an ending. Then the train lurched and began to move, so suddenly that everyone stumbled and there were more screams.

Before we'd even left the yard, the straight cons had their shivs out and started shoving their way through the crowd. Someone on the other side of the car played the hero and got cut. The cons had a good system, almost as if they'd done this before. Two or three would gang up on one victim and beat him up or stab him while the others formed a ring facing outwards with their knives. In this way they were able to terrify everyone on the train (who were, for the most part, terrified anyway) and soon they were roaming individually and taking whatever they wanted.

"Gimme your watch," one of them said to me.

I silently handed over my wristwatch.

"And your wallet."

I gave him that too, and asked: "You want my PIN? You think there's going to be any ATMs, where we're going?"

The con, a tall and stupid white boy with the high domed forehead of a cretin, gave me a malicious look and turned around to rob someone else. The crowd surged as someone was beaten on the far side of the car.

The train rattled on the tracks. We were still moving very slowly. I had a sudden memory of taking the GO train home every Friday to go back to Oakville for the weekends during dental school. The child beside me was weeping and holding his mother's hand. He'd soiled his pants.

It took the cons almost an hour to move through the train and steal everything they wanted. We were moving much more quickly now, the sound of the tracks clanking rhythmically beneath our feet, the train swaying gently side to side, when they started to rape the girl.

I don't know how old she was. Truth be told, I never even saw her. I just felt another one of those pulses move through the crowd that signified another struggle, the wave of people moving that you couldn't resist, that would have put you on your ass if there'd been room enough to fall, and then I heard the girl start to scream.

At first the screaming girl sounded terrified, but in a queer sort of way, hopeful. I guess a large part of the reason people scream when they get hurt or scared or in trouble is that someone will hear and come and help. Because normally, that's what people do. But plenty of people heard this girl scream, and I didn't see one person twitch. Not one. I mean, what percentage of people in life do you think are heroes? Ten? Five? One? There should have been at least one hero on the train, right? But everyone stood there, too ashamed to make eye contact with anyone else, shifting their weight from foot to foot, silent.

And then the girl's scream changed a little, into a wail, or a moan, or a species of agonized sobbing, as if she suddenly became cognizant of her situation, as if she realized that no one was coming to help.

Suddenly I had a terrible thought. What if, I thought, the reason was that there were no heroes on this train was that because all the heroes were already dead? What if the kind of people who would stand up to a gang of rapists were the same kind of people who would refuse to denounce their neighbours, to confess to crimes that they had not committed, to meekly get on the train to the labour camp? What if there were no heroes on this train because no hero would ever end up on this train?

The girl's screaming changed in tone again, this time I'm not exactly sure how except that it was more unendurable, and I became aware that the straight cons were laughing. And I tell you as truly as anything I have ever said in this life that I didn't want to live any more, I didn't want to take one more breath if I had to feel like such a coward, but that there was still some sort of force that prevented me from moving other than fear for my life. And I think it was the combined cowardice of everyone else in the train, if that makes any sense. There was this tremendous silent force radiating out that made it feel that to try to stop what was happening would be somehow incredibly gauche, stupid, or rude, because it would force everyone to acknowledge that it was happening at all.

I saw the child looking at his shoes, like everyone else, and smelt the stink from the shit in his pants. I did not make a conscious decision. I suddenly found that I was forcing my way through the crowd.

The straight cons knew I was coming, of course. They could feel it, in the shifting movements of the mob that had been heretofore as still as the grave.

Two of them stepped forward into the little empty space that separated them from the rest of the passengers. One was tall and fat, with a grotesquely stubbled double chin and crooked, oversized yellow teeth. The other was small and lithe with obscene blue tattoos curling around his neck. They both had knives. I went for the small one.

He started to say something, to make some threat, and that was his mistake. He let me make the first move when I was in too close for him to react. I grabbed his knife hand and twisted it behind his back so it dropped on to the rubber mat. Then I slipped behind him and applied a rear naked choke. That is, I wrapped my left arm around his neck so my elbow was under his chin and used my left hand to grab my right bicep while I jammed my right elbow into the con's back and put my right hand on the back of his head. Squeezing this choke cuts off the blood to the brain and causes unconsciousness within seconds.

I started pulling the con back into the crowd as quickly as I could. He was gripping my elbow with his empty hands and making a gurgling sound. His fat buddy with the buck teeth tried to lunge in and stab me, but I tucked my head down into my con's neck and didn't give him much of a target. The other cons started shouting and pressing forward and everyone else was screaming and scrambling to get out of the way. It was like being in the middle of a riot.

No one was helping me. We could have overwhelmed those fuckers in an instant. Not one person raised a hand. Then again, I hadn't tried to help anyone up until now either.

Two of the cons were struggling closest to me. One was the bucktoothed one, the other was a dirty looking old man, balding on top with a greasy ponytail lying on his neck like the pelt of a dead animal. They weren't stabbing wildly any more but just looking to close in and finish the job. They were going to be able to do it in just a couple of seconds, too. But then Bucktooth, who was on the right, suddenly raised his eyebrows and widened his eyes, like he'd seen something very surprising. It reminded me, for some reason, of the look on Pepe Le Pew's face when his gaze fell upon a black cat who, through some misadventure, has had a white stripe painted down her back.

A sharpened screwdriver had been driven into the side of his neck and it came out again with the speed of the needle on a sewing machine. An arterial spurt of blood squirted across the car.

The mullet-head con had just enough time to glance over at his companion before the hammer struck him on the forehead with the force of a thunderbolt. Again I noticed the change in his eyes. One moment they were on the same level, and the next, one was substantially lower than the other. There was also a very dark and red section of his head where stuff seemed to be pressing out.

The two cons slumped down to the ground at roughly the same moment, sliding slowly through the press of the crowd, smearing blood everywhere. The mullet-head con was jittering nervously.

Both the screwdriver and the hammer had been wielded by the same man, a tremendously tall and heavy black fellow with bulging muscular arms that were almost ripping through his thin, ragged white t-shirt. His hair was done up in thick, almost clotted dreadlocks that jutted out of his head at disgusting angles, giving him the air of a cactus coated in shit.

His back was to me. I heard him bellow one word at the gang of cons swarming on me. The word was: "What?"

The cons came to a halt.

"That's what I thought," the questioner said in a thick Caribbean accent.

The cons shifted, a little unsure of themselves. One of them, also black, but as thin as a reed, called out to me: "We'll fucking see you in the camps, bitch."

The questioner (whom I shall call Wilder) turned to look at me. His features were blunt and large, with a crooked nose (broken and healed many times over) and cauliflower ears that jutted out perpendicular to his skull. But the most striking thing about him was his eyes, which were a blue so faded and worn that they were almost grey, like old jeans or an overcast sky. They gave him a strangely distant quality, as if he was observing everything he saw from a very long way away.

"You gonna let that boy go?" he asked.

I realized that I was still choking the con, who had long since stopped struggling. His face was ashen grey. I quickly let him go and his body slumped down to the ground. He was dead. I had killed a man for the first time, without even knowing I was doing it.

*****

It was a twenty-four hour train ride from Toronto to Gull River 55. That include five or six hours sitting dead still in the train yard outside of Hurkett. More and more people just started to let go in their pants. The heat was oppressive, the stench unbearable. Many passed out from exhaustion or hunger and thirst. Everyone was miserable and afraid.

When the train finally did come to a halt, and that whistle screamed out again, you could feel the relief in the air, which was absurd, considering where we were going.

The door slid open and the cold air howled in like a swarm of locusts. I was wearing a thin cotton suit and the wind cut through it like it wasn't there. Outside the light was blinding. I saw that there were guards everywhere, dogs straining on their leashes and barking savagely. Past them were the buildings of the camp, the long low huts where I assumed the prisoners slept, and the smaller detached cottages for the guards. Past everything were the trees, tall and dark green and endless in every direction.

I knew something was a terribly wrong the moment I saw the prisoners, off in the distance, though the chain metal fence that separated the train yard from the main camp. They were much too thin. I had never seen anyone so thin in my life. They moved spider-like up against the fence, lifting their feet high to make their way through the deep snow. They were close to death.

Wilder was standing near the base of the ramp. Like me, he was looking at the prisoners on the other side of his face. The expression on his face was difficult to read.

I could see my frozen breath in front of my face. The guards were shouting at us and dividing us up into groups. I lined up with a group of people and we were marched off across the frozen ground through the high gates and into an enormous building constructed out of sheet metal that served as a massive processing centre.

We formed rough lines and passed through different stations. Our fingerprints were taken and they asked us questions and took notes and roughly etched numbers on our skin. It was all a dumb show I think, a performance, to make us think that we were still being watched, recorded. To make us believe that we were still within the protective embrace of a state, of some sort of association of men, however harsh and vindictive, when the simple truth was we had moved outside of the bounds of any human jurisdiction.

I am, as I said, a religious man, and so I found it then a little peculiar how perturbed I was to have no interposing layer of human authority between myself and God. Like I was somehow naked and exposed under His watchful eye. As if we were glossy beetles and albino worms squirming in the sunlight after a rock had been lifted by an inquiring child. Rather than mercy and love, I felt from Him a majestic and sublime indifference, an unknowableness. A powerful sense of some strange and incomprehensible machinery from which I had been heretofore shielded but which had underpinned all my life and all its works were now laid bare before my eyes.

We were separated into groups, men, women and children, and then stripped of our clothes and possessions. They roughly cut our hair down to our scalps in spite of the cold and rushed us through the showers. We were dusted with some sort of powder and issued rough and heavy identical jumpsuits that felt as if they were stitched together from the hides of cacti.

Eventually we found ourselves kneeling, row upon row in the snow, in a wide parade ground across from the longhouses where we were to sleep. Guards pacing among us with machineguns dangling on new leather straps from their shoulders. A temporary stage erected in front of us upon which the commandant was making a speech. It seemed more targeted towards those who believed they're been relocated than the prisoners. The salient point was that there was a nickel mine near the camp and we would be working there. I turned my head and saw a troop of men coming back from the pits. They were so thin and listless and devoid of light or hope that they didn't even seem human. We, the new arrivals, stared at them, but the guards paid them no mind nor did the workers themselves seem to understand their extraordinary state.

The cold leached into my bones. I could feel the blood draining out of my extremities; they were going white before my eyes. Many of the people around me were beginning to tremble. One or two began to cough.

Eventually we were allowed to stand and we made our way to the longhouses. Inside was as cold as out, only sheltered from the wind and more damp. I came to my assigned bunk and found that it contained an emaciated corpse that had been stripped naked.

I stood for a while, wondering what to do, and then I dragged it outside and dumped it in the snow.

*****

Man, as Dostoevsky wrote, truly is a thing that can get used to anything. Just as we can adjust to the greatest luxury and good fortune, so can the most inhuman torments slowly transform into a dull routine. So that in the end it is apathy and despair, and not pain and suffering, that pose the greatest threat to the spirit of the resident of the concentration camp.

There were three main torments in the camp: hunger, exhaustion, and the cold.

We were woken every morning by screaming sirens long, long before dawn (it was dark very late in Gull River 55 in October). We would shuffle out of our huts in our meagre winter clothing into the freezing black morning for roll call. It usually seemed to be snowing. The senior prisoners (or capos, most of whom were righteous cons) would strike us into line. We were issued our ration of bread for the morning, and then we would be called out by number and assigned to a work detail.

We were working for Jien Canada Mining, a subsidiary of Jilin Jien Nickel Industry Company of China. The open pit of the mine was about a kilometre to the west of the camp. So we would march in a huge pack down the road, clumped together, shivering, trying not to collapse. When we arrived we would be forced to perform any number of exhausting forms of manual labour. Many of them involved shovelling show, but we also dug ditches, cleaned latrines, and hauled loads of timber, rock, or dirt. All under the direction of Chinese mining engineers in their thick jackets (which looked to be coated in Teflon and stuffed with goose down) with the guards and their machineguns lurking in the background.

There were three breaks during the work day. One at mid-morning, a few hours after the sun made its appearance, watery and low in the sky. One at noon, when we were issued another ration, about a pint of watery soup. And one in the afternoon, when the temperature (always cold) was beginning to plummet like a stone.

We walked back to the camp at night, where we were issued more bread. If any of us had Jien coupons, there might be a short period of time to redeem them before the canteen closed. Afterwards, we would return to our beds.

The bread was gassy and spongy, white and bland and devoid of nutrients. Some saved their ration, only eating a mouthful now and again through the morning. I did not ascribe to this school. I wolfed my bread down immediately, in the not unjustified fear that someone might steal it.

The soup we were issued for lunch tasted as if it was made by boiling dirt. The guards went around with a large metal pot held between them and issued every prisoner a cup. I remember how I used to watch the ladle swirl around through the stone-coloured liquid and how I prayed to all the Gods in heaven that the guard would dip the spoon to the bottom of the pot to come up with some peas, noodles, meat, something. More often than not they just skimmed off some broth from the top.

I never thought so much about food in my life. Every waking moment was dominated by dreams of food. I thought especially of all the fast food I had turned my nose up at. McDonald's, for instance. Now what had been so bad about McDonald's? Or Burger King. Wendy's. Harvey's. And that's not even counting the more upscale burger joints, like say your Hero Burger or your South Side Burger Co. Their names would dance through my head as I attempt to drive a pickaxe into the frozen ground again and again, only to have it bounce away and jar my emaciated arms all the way up to my shoulder and perhaps to hear the derisive laughter or a shouted threat of a guard.

My body wasted before my eyes. I didn't get thin the way you got thin if you went on a diet. It's not like I just lost my gut or my ass got smaller. My thighs shrunk. Down to the bone. They didn't even look like thighs any more, not the way thighs looked on any person I'd ever seen before. Bones jutted out of my hips and shoulders. Ribs came out clean and distinct, little canyons in weak pale flesh. My face grew lean and angular like a skull and my eyes loomed big and wide and dead.

I was tired all the time. When I wasn't working I used to just sit and stare at nothing. The cold crawled inside me, under my skin, so I almost forgot about it. The white stiff fingers that fumbled and refused to do what you told them, the numb feet you could barely feel, the pain deep in your joints, the wracking cough. It all just became part of the furniture. But even so, you never quite did get accustomed to it. It was like a needle, jabbing away at you, keeping you from finding a moment of peace.

The prisoners would congregate at places of warmth. Near a light, a fire, a heater, a ray of sunshine. Nothing seemed to work. At best it warmed you up on the outside, a little, before someone shouted at you to move along. The warmth never quite got all the way inside you, it never seemed to touch you where you really were.

The death rate, as you can imagine, was quite enormous. From hypothermia, from frostbite, from the flu, from accidents in the field. But it seemed to me, perhaps wrongly, that the greatest cause of death was simple and ordinary despair. Every morning there would be one or two prisoners who would simply refuse to rise from their beds. If they had friends, someone might try to cajole them out to work. Nothing would work; not blows, not threats, not desperate entreaties, not even tears, if someone could manage to squeeze a few out. The doomed lay still and naked and unblinking while we walked out into the dark of morning, and when their number was called and they were not present, the guards would head inside and find them and pronounce the dreaded word:
"Infirmary."

For in the infirmary there was no work, and if there was no work, then the prisoner received half rations, and swiftly died.

I saw all manner of horrors. Fingers and toes black and wizened with frostbite plucked off and thrown in the snow. Children with distended bellies lying in their own uncontrolled filth like famine-struck villagers in Africa. Cold brittle bones snapped and jutting through the skin after an industrial accident. An endless parade of beatings. Some few blatant executions. I hauled corpses down frozen roads and stacked them like cordwood in great piles and wondered when it would be my turn to join them.

The Chinese were completely unconcerned with our fate. They gave directions through the working day then retired to their own camp in the evening. Our tormentors were divided into two groups; the guards and the senior prisoners (or "capos.") Of these two, the capos were more openly sadistic. They had been selected for their position based on their cruelty and genuinely enjoyed causing us misery. Furthermore, if they did not enforce the rules with zealous inhumanity, they were soon demoted back down to our ranks.

The guards were just as cruel as the capos, and more dangerous, since they could actually kill us with impunity. However, their hostility towards us was tempered with contempt. If a capo caught you resting for a moment, he would usually strike you with a shovel. A guard would normally only bark an order, or perhaps hit you with a snowball. We weren't worth getting angry over. We were numerous, fungible, expendable, ephemeral. But most of all, we were contemptible.

I sometimes wondered, like we all used to, how the guards in the concentration camps of long ago and far away (Germany, Russia, Cambodia) could have been so cruel towards their fellow human beings. The answer is two-fold. The first is that concentration guards are specifically selected for their sadism. The second is that residents of concentration camps are not human beings.

We're physically disgusting, first of all. We're grotesquely thin; we're always coughing up great gobs of bloody phlegm. But it's more than just how we looked. Because we were in danger, you see, because it was so difficult to survive, it meant you had to do everything you possibly could. You had to be utterly subservient, scurrying to obey the orders of the Chinese, guards, and even capos. Even one word back could mean the end of your life. You had to plead and beg, pathetically, to be served your soup from the bottom of the bowl. You had to weep and scream to save a scrap of mouldy bread. You could not share your rations with someone less fortunate than you.

If so much as a potato became available, you had to be ready to kill. It was not uncommon to see two prisoners come to blows over the shoes on a corpse. If the guards were looking for volunteers to work the overnight shift, you had to do anything you could to keep your number off the list, no matter if it meant someone else's number would replace yours.

There were prisoners, of course, who spoke honourably to the guards, who refused to be craven worms, who were kind and generous and kept their pride, who encouraged their fellows and who shared their bread. Who would not try to survive if it meant they had to plant a knife in the back of one of their fellows. Those prisoners died.

What did it say of us who were left?

These thoughts bounced around in my head, day after monotonous day, when I could drag my mind from food for a few moments. But their truth never struck me forcefully until one fateful morning when I was walking to work in a large crowd.

As I've said, it was a long cold walk in the dark to the work site and it could be a dangerous trip. It was not uncommon for prisoners to stumble, from exhaustion or hunger or numb feet or ice, and we marched so tightly up against one another that a number of us could fall at once. When this happened, the guards would beat us mercilessly. Such a beating might very well make one unfit for work, which would mean the infirmary, which would mean death.

This meant that it was safest to be in the middle of the crowd. First, it was warmest; second, one was furthest from the truncheons of the capos and the rifle-butts of the guards. And so there was a constant battle between the prisoners, as we walked, to worm our way towards the centre of our group, a battle both secret (since we were desperate to not attract attention to ourselves) and desperate (since our lives might very well depend on it).

My health was holding up well and I am a strong man and I usually managed to have a barrier of my fellows between me and our tormentors. But one day, one morning seemingly unlike any other, I had a revelation. I was engaged in a joust with a tall man. He had inside position on me but I was strong and remorseless and a little closer to the ground than him and I was successfully pushing inside of him when I looked up and saw a guard watching us, smoking a cigarette, with an amused look on his fat demon's face.

And I thought of how I must look to him; shoving another man out from the warmth, to be beaten instead of me. All of a sudden I was washed over with hatred for myself, for still being alive, after all these months. They had managed to kill everything good inside of me, so thoroughly that I could barely remember any other life. They had transformed me into something that I could not honestly say deserved to live.

I stopped struggling with the taller man and I was pushed aside. A number of other prisoners saw their opportunity and thrust past me. I was shoved to the side. I looked at the prisoners with their bald heads and frost-bitted faces and bony shoulders and repulsive, selfish eyes and I thought of baby birds thrusting their heads out of the nest. Thinking only of themselves.

I moved all the way to the edge of the group and slipped on ice and fell to the side. I was struck across the shoulders and cursed, I did not see by whom. The prisoners did not look back. They marched on, saving themselves.

I rose to my feet and walked on grimly, slightly apart from the herd. At lunch I saw a man, younger than twenty-five, spill his soup while coughing wretchedly. I gave him half of mine. The look on his face would break your heart.

The only way to survive up at Gull River 55 was to allow them to transform you into something that was no longer a human being. Something that was just a set of reflexes geared at self-preservation. It seemed to me, at the time, that this was their ultimate victory. And so I privately resolved to die, as quickly as I could.

*****

A few days after making this resolution I was standing in formation with the rest of my work detail, shivering in the morning darkness, and waiting to hear what my responsibilities for the day would be. A group of three capos sauntered over towards us. I did not recognize them, at the time, but they certainly recognized me. Their leader was a short, wiry man with a nasty squint who was missing a few teeth. He came up to me and smiled and whispered:
"You're dead."

To give you an idea of the scale of the operation at Gull River 55, it had been five months and I had yet run into any of the straight cons with whom I had shared the train from Toronto, at least not to my knowledge. Most of them had been assigned easier work duties on the other side of the camp. But they had not forgotten about me and they knew where I was now.

I looked through my persecutor the way only a dead man can, and then turned away and shrugged. He didn't like that and let me know it by smacking a truncheon just below my ear. It hit some hard, bony spot and pain lit through my skull. I dropped to the ground and they hit me a few more times but then backed off. Capos couldn't just beat a prisoner to death for no reason, not when there was work to be done. They quickly moved off and I eventually rolled onto my knees and lifted my head. A guard barked an order at me and I managed to stand.

That night I saw them watching me as I stood in line to receive my evening bread. I wolfed it down quickly, almost while I was still in line, and made my way back towards the longhouse where I slept. They came up around to me and one of them took my arm. "If you make a sound," he said, "I'll stab you."

I felt a knife jab into my ribs. My response was to lift my right leg so high that my knee almost touched my chin and drive it down into his foot. I felt a bone crack under my heel and the capo screamed. The knife went away for an instant and I bolted forward. They caught up to me right by the door.

I let out a cry as one of them tackled me from behind. My head bumped up against the wood of the longhouse and everything doubled in my vision. I tried to turn around onto my back but it was impossible with one of them lying on me. A boot stomped down into the back of my head and my face smashed into the frozen earth, bending my neck at an unhealthy angle. The knife stabbed into my side, luckily digging into a rib and getting stuck. Kicks rained in, savagely, from every direction. I felt something inside my left forearm snap.

Someone had his arms wrapped around my head and he was lifting me off the ground. They were trying to press my mouth down on the step to the longhouse, presumably so they could split my head in half by stomping on it. I was getting my right arm into the hold and squirming my head loose and turning it to the side. They were all kicking me and I felt something in my knee pop. More hands started gripping onto my head. Everything was silent and very serious.

A machine gun tat-tat-tatted and I fell down into the snow with a tremendous weight pressing on me. I screamed as my broken arm shifted. I was covered in something hot and wet.

The shrill whistle of the guards.

"Break it up!" someone bellowed. "Break it the fuck up, you maggots!"

The weight lifted off my back, slightly. It felt as if one or two people were still lying on me.

"What are you doing, man?" one of the capos shrieked.

"Did you just talk back to me?" the guard shouted. "Did you just fucking talk back to me?"

A moment of silence, then a surprised laugh.

"Are you capos? Ha ha! Your hats fell off! Ha ha!"

The longhouse was raised slightly off the ground and I now started squirming away from the bodies, underneath into the cobwebbed dark.

None of the capos said a word to the guard. He was still laughing.

"Well, what the fuck? Serves you right for ganging up on him, you fucking pussies. Take those bodies away and stack them with the rest."

The pain radiating from my left arm was resplendent. The knife was still sticking out of my ribs and my knee was pulsing in agony along with the beat of my heart. I managed to slip away under the longhouse just as the corpse was lifted off of me.

"Ha ha ha!" the guard laughed behind me. "Look at him go!"

When I got a little ways under the longhouse I stopped moving and jerked the knife out of my side. The pain made me scream, high and quavering. I bled into the ground and gasped for air and shivered inside my damp clothing. Dust and grit kept getting in my mouth and lungs. I thought of my life just a year ago. Cleaning teeth, asking kids what flavour of fluoride they wanted, going to the gym and coming home to the smell of my wife's cooking and the sight of my lazy sister sprawled on the couch reading the poetry of Jorge Luis Borges. I knew that I'd never get any of it back and I cried into the dirt, great whooping sobs coming from some deep place inside me as dark as the morning in Gull River 55. I almost didn't crawl back out from under the longhouse but in the end I did.

Everyone on their bunks saw my enormous limp, the way that I cradled my arm close to my chest, the blood and dirt all over me. No one said a word. I crawled into my bed and lay there, unsleeping, until the whistle sounded. When I tried to sit up I found that I was stuck to my bed with frozen blood. I felt like a broken thermos; all full of jangling glass. When I dropped down to the ground my knee gave way and I pitched onto my face and wheezed in pain.

I stood up and staggered out into the morning. Bright white snowflakes, flashing with moonlight. I fell into line and stood at the edge while the cold crept up my pant legs. This was it. I was going to die. I swayed a little on my feet. I did not feel anything at all. I put my bread in my pocket. I had no appetite.

When my number was called I marched the long march to the mining camp, right on the edge of the group, cut to the core with the wind, slipping from time to time. At the work site I was assigned a trench to dig with a few other prisoners. I lifted the pickaxe with one hand and tried to drive it into the earth. It bounced off and skipped into a snowbank. I was trying to dig it out when I felt someone's presence behind me.

I looked over my shoulder. The guard was bemused. "Infirmary," was all he said.

*****

In the infirmary we lay shoulder to skinny shoulder on a dirt floor in a lean-to made of corrugated iron. It should have been cold but it wasn't, due to the mass of human bodies. Our caregivers were fellow prisoners. They made a splint for my broken arm with a piece of wood. There was nothing else they could do for me, since the only medication they had was aspirin and it was saved for more desperate cases than mine.

I drank a cup of watery soup in the morning and in the evening. I only stood up when I needed to use the toilet. Otherwise I slept or stared at the ceiling. Around me people screamed and wept. The stink was so overwhelming it felt difficult to breathe.

I'm not sure what would have happened to me if things had been allowed to run their course. Overall I was very miserable and I did not want to live any longer. But then again, I no longer wished to die. I felt disconnected from the whole universe, a fixture come loose, rattling around, without purpose.

After three days in the infirmary two guards came inside and called my name. I tried to sit up but couldn't. They lifted me, not roughly, to my feet and draped a blanket over my shoulder. Then they brought me outside to a skidoo.

"Hold on tight," one of the guards told me.

I sat behind him as we blasted through the camp and out onto the road that led to the nickel mine. The wind was as sharp as a knife so I buried my face in the guard's jacket and just held on with my good arm. I was not, in the least, curious where we were going. I assumed it was somewhere terrible. I felt utterly numb.

We stopped after ten minutes or so and I lifted my head. At first I had no idea where we were. It was like our camp, but better. The long-houses were made of metal and looked like the trailers movie stars would live in. There were no guards or electric fences or piles of corpses. Everything was neat and orderly.

Suddenly, in a blinding flash of hallucinatory clarity, I knew what had happened. I was dead, and this was heaven. Heaven was a slightly nicer concentration camp.

Then the door to one of the steel trailers slid open and I saw a Chinese man in a sleek-looking Nike fleece and I knew I was just in the Chinese camp.

"What's going on?" I said to the guard.

"You a dentist, ain't you?"

"Pardon me?"

"The Chinese dentist, well, he had an accident."

The guard smiled. He was clearly enjoying my confusion. "I guess one of 'em has a toothache."

The trailer contained a room stocked with all the equipment a dentist would need. There was a chair, a light, racks of tools, cabinets filled with floss and different flavours of fluoride. There was a tube of nitrous oxide and an x-ray machine. Everything spotless and white. I had to touch the light to make sure it was real. I felt like I was a million miles away.

There was a sound behind me. A Chinese man came in, corpulent and malevolent, with psychotic eyes. Accident indeed. I bowed my head a little.

He spoke to me in Chinese, harshly. I looked past him to the guard, who grinned and shrugged.

"I don't speak Chinese," I said.

The Chinese man shouted, spit flying out of his mouth, and I could see that his teeth were black and rotten. I stepped forward and put my fingers in his mouth. He started and tried to jerk away but I had a hold of his bottom jaw. Several of his back molars were impacting and he had some nasty cavities. I took my hand away.

I looked into those mad, dancing amber eyes and I pointed at the chair and said: "Sit."

The Chinese man took a deep breath and was about to speak.

"Do you think," I said, "that shouting at me will make your teeth hurt less? Do you think there are any more dentists here to help you if you don't do what I say?"

He hesitated. He could speak a little English after all. Of course he could. I was patient, but not too patient, unafraid to die. The Chinese man sat down with all the dignity he could muster.

After I put gloves on my hands (with some difficulty, considering my fractured arm) I went for the nitrous oxide. At first he resisted but I made it clear I would not proceed unless he was anathematized. He shouted at me once or twice but I just rocked back on my heels and waited. I noticed that he was wearing a gun. Well, I thought, let him shoot me then. Then he can keep his toothache.

Eventually he sat back and folded his arms and I gave him the gas. His mouth opened and I looked around his teeth with the mirror. Ghastly. I poked his gums with the sickle probe and a shot of pus blurted out. I mopped it up with a cotton wool roll and then I gave him some local anaesthetic.

I put a saliva injector in his mouth so I could see what I was doing and then I quickly pulled three of his molars, so smoothly that he didn't feel a thing. There was blood and pus everywhere but I managed to suck them up with the saliva injector or wipe them away with cotton. I stitched shut the gaping holes in his gums, a neat trick with only one hand.

Then I went to work with the drill, scraping away the decayed sections of his remaining teeth. It was difficult and I knew if I made one slip I would die. But I didn't feel any pressure, none in the slightest. I was so happy to be a dentist again. It made me feel as if I was re-establishing who I was, reclaiming something that was stolen from me.

I was at it for almost an hour with the drill, and applying the restorative material took almost another. When I was finished I had completely rebuilt his mouth.

When I looked over at the guard I saw that he was gone but there were two Chinese men watching me.

"Tell him he needs antibiotics," I said.

Then a strange feeling swam through my head and I knew I was going to faint.

*****

I stayed at the Chinese camp for two weeks and I gave everyone a check up. At the end of the two week period I was sent back to the main camp and performed the same function for all of the guards and for a few privileged prisoners (mostly the mistresses of certain senior camp officials). Afterwards, I was sent to work in the infirmary, where I wandered through the rows of the sick and dying dispensing the occasional half-tablet of aspirin.

We were granted better rations, mainly more bread and soup and the occasional treat, such as a piece of cheese or sausage or chocolate. Many of my former tormentors ate with me but I paid them little mind and they me. Perhaps they felt they'd proved their point. Perhaps they'd never really been angry with me to begin with and had only been picking on me out of a sense of professionalism.

It was at this time that I saw Wilder again, who was now a capo, of course. Every morning he would nod his head to me and amiably say: "What's up, Doc?" Then he would often steal a piece of bread off of my plate. Wilder stole from everyone. Anything he wanted, he took. He was the only capo I ever saw stand up to the guards. He wouldn't talk back to them, but only give them a look so frankly homicidal and so deeply insane while pulling himself up to his full height that even the most domineering guards would find an excuse to leave him alone.

We privileged prisoners who were not capos always sat a little apart from them during breakfast. We mostly worked in the infirmary or were domestics to the guards. Some few prisoners made the hike to the Chinese camp and performed various tasks there. There were also those who worked in the kitchens and would come join us towards the end of our meals to smoke a cigarette or to tell some black joke, smiling like ghouls.

The last group of privileged prisoners were the mistresses. They did not eat with us. I saw them sometimes in the barracks or around the cabins. Most of them would not meet my gaze, though some would stare at me insolently. I was eventually told not to make eye contact with them by a sergeant. Apparently they had complained about me.

I do not want to overstate the conditions for the so-called "privileged" prisoners. We still did not get enough food. We still worked ceaselessly, and our work (such as hauling corpses) could still be tremendously physically exhausting. It was still terribly cold. Almost all of us had wretched coughs that wracked us through the day and night. The mortality rate was much lower, but every day the faces around the breakfast table changed.

And it started to grow difficult for me to work around the sick, because it was becoming so easy. Every day I told them there was no medicine, no food, no help. I started to hate them, their constant demands and their whimpering pleas, or worse yet, their dull apathy, their gutless surrender, their lack of dignity. I grew so accustomed to the corpses I could drag one all the way across the camp, alternatively carrying, rolling and kicking it, without ever once feeling like I was handling something that had once been a human being.

It was during one of these trips that I was suddenly aware of what I was doing. A woman had died with her arm sticking out from her body. By the time we realized she was dead, rigor mortis had set in and it was as if she was carved from stone. It was hell dragging her to the corpse pile because there was just no way to do it properly. She kept jerking out of my hands and then I'd look at her, her stupid face staring at nothing, so hatefully thin and weak, and I got so angry I could hardly see, so filled with rage, and I fell to my knees and started bending her arm as hard as I could, trying to break it or rip it off so she'd be easier to drag through the snow.

I heard someone cry out and when I looked up I saw a child running away, darting between two longhouses and disappear. I didn't see clearly who it was. It didn't matter, really. What mattered, again, was what had happened to me. How everything decent inside me had died.

I sat there, in the snow, on my knees, for a while. My breath making a warm cloud around my bearded face. My body coated with grime, my skinny ribs falling in and out, some kind of dark buzzing in my brain.

I thought again of how I simply should not be living like this, of how my own weakness and cowardice had led me here, and of how the same weakness and cowardice spread throughout the heart of man had allowed this insane situation to come about. We had all had choices, all of us, and it was something in me that had led me here, to this point, grunting and straining to break off the arm of a corpse in Gull River 55. I could not blame anyone else. The whole thing was a diorama of my heart.

Over the next few weeks things grew more difficult in the camps. The trains kept coming, coming, coming, and the camp got more and more overcrowded. Eventually our rations were cut so that they were just as inadequate as they had been before. I can't imagine how they must have been for the ordinary prisoners, but I knew they were starving. There were one or two explosions of violence. It was then that Wilder approached me about the escape.

*****

"You're crazy," I said wearily.

Wilder grinned at me. He didn't deny it.

"Ain't nothing crazy about it," Muddy said. He was a tall spindly man with slick black hair and a few missing teeth in the corner of his smile. Muddy worked as a cleaner at the Chinese camp, but he had a reputation as a real hard case. "Only crazy thing would be to stay here."

We were huddled between two of the longhouses, for the moment out of the sight of the guards. If they saw us like this, we'd be in trouble. It was frowned upon to have private conversations, to congregate in small groups. It must have been March or April by this time.

"We're all privileged," I said.

"Don't be a cunt," Muddy said. "It don't mean shit."

"How long you think till they get a real dentist up here?" Wilder said. "I figure in the spring. Don't you?"

"Forget a real dentist," Muddy said. "How many dentists you think come here on the train every damn day? Shit, son. They're bringing more people here than they's food for. They coming every day. It ain't just these po' fuckers that are gonna feel the pinch. It's us too. You think we're special?"

"No," I said.

"We got to go," Muddy said. "I heard the guards talking. Said in one of the longhouses they stopped reporting when people die. Fucking cannibalism bro. That's where we're at."

Wilder glanced at Muddy briefly with a surprised look on his face. Then he looked back at me and exhaled a soft white cloud around his bearded mouth.

"How the fuck are we going to do it?" I asked.

"Simple man," Wilder said. "Go cross the lake."

"Walk right across to Rocky Bay," Muddy said.

"How far is that?" I asked.

Wilder looked at Muddy, who shrugged.

"About 100 kliks."

"Jesus," I said.

"We got to go, bro," Wilder said. "Lake thaws soon. Then the bugs come. We'll be trapped here. We won't make it another year."

"They might even start executing us, Doc," Muddy said. "Who knows? Just fucking shoot us all."

I lifted my hands and breathed on them. "And then where are we supposed to go? After? We hit Rocky Bay, then what?"

"Anything's better than here," Muddy said.

"You really don't have much imagination," I said, "do you?"

"Shit doc," Wilder said. "What the fuck is up with you? We came talk to you cause I thought for sure you'd be down. Way you took on those old boys on the train. What the fuck did they do to you, you want to stay here now? They really got to you, didn't they? You up in here six months they got you all turned around."

There hadn't really been any question in my mind. Not really. I used to have those sort of fake debates with myself. You know what I mean; you're deciding whether to go out and meet your friends at the bar all the way downtown or to sit in front of your laptop watching old UFC fights on Youtube and eating popcorn. You pretend to be weighing the pros and cons, but really, you already know.

And if there had been a question, Wilder's words would have answered it. Because they were true. I had already changed so much, betrayed every principle I had. A few short months ago I had been physically unable to listen to that poor girl scream without going to help her. Now I saw and heard worse things every day and didn't feel a thing. They'd gotten to me somehow, despite all my resolutions. It had sapped my faith in myself more than I cared to admit. There was no way, I realized, that I could pass up on a chance to get that back. It was, simply, worth dying for.

"Well Wilder," I said, "if you're gonna twist my arm ..."

*****

We weren't able to steal any food, because we were watched far too closely. We just had to store the bread we were getting, which was hard since we weren't getting enough food to being with.

We fled the camp at night, when it was dark, before we were to go to bed. We just headed out to the train tracks and followed them to the south, the snow crunching under our feet. A narrow path slashed unnaturally straight through the dark forest. It was surprisingly bright with the reflected moonlight from the snow.

After we'd travelled about a kilometre we left the train tracks and headed to the west through the deep snow. It was here that it became extremely difficult to travel. It had started to warm up and the layers of ice in the snow banks were weakened. It was not uncommon for a leg to plunge through, so that we were half-walking on the snow, and half ploughing through it. It was especially difficult for Wilder, who was often out of breath.

Even to travel a few hundred metres was like running a marathon. Despite the freezing cold, sweat was trickling down my face and back under my hood. I could taste blood whenever I coughed. The woods were empty except for us.

We did not reach the lake until dawn. All of a sudden there it was: the thick evergreen forest suddenly ended, and we were at a rocky shore, leading out onto a desert of pure white with the sky in the east only now just bruising with the sun. The lake stretched on forever.

"We gotta keep moving," Wilder said.

"I need to rest," I said.

"Later," Wilder said. "We gotta go while the sun's up."

And so we dropped down into the snow on the lake, all of us sinking down to our hips and having to drag ourselves back out to move. We'd walk a few steps, then fall through again. The sun came up over the horizon and set the snow on fire.

At noon we ate a little of what we had.

"How many days have we got to go?"

Wilder shrugged. "Ten klicks a day, ten days."

I didn't reply. It was just so half-assed, somehow. Was our whole escape going to be blown for lack of food? Couldn't we have done something? It was such a predictable way to die.

We kept walking. Soon my legs were cut and bruised from crashing through the snow. My fingers and toes were white and numb and I couldn't feel my face from the wind howling across the ice. As the sun was setting behind us we stopped to dig out a shelter in the snow on a small rocky island.

We crawled inside and lay shoulder to shoulder. At first I was cold, almost freezing. Eventually it warmed and I slept. When I awoke it was unpleasantly hot and I was soaked through with sweat.

The next day I couldn't stop coughing, and when I did I could taste copper in my mouth. My head grew light and my body grew heavy. I had to look at things for a long time before I actually saw them. At lunchtime, I looked at my little handful of bread for fifteen minutes before I put it in my mouth, only to find it surprisingly difficult to chew. Sometimes, when I had to pull myself out of the snow, I thought I would be physically unable to do so. The same way I could not uproot a tree with my bare hands; the same level of impossibility.

The night after the third day I came outside our shelter in the middle of the night and was stunned to see the aurora borealis ranging across the sky. The Northern Lights. I'd seen them before in the camps, of course, but I don't think they'd ever been so spectacular. It looked as if the air had caught fire. And for the first time in my life, I wished I wasn't a dentist, I wish I'd gotten an arts degree like my sister, so I'd have the words to make that sight last longer than I will. My god it was so beautiful. It was green and red and blue, somehow all at the same time, sheeted together, moving back and forth, curling like smoke, shimmering like a mirage. Tears trickled down my cheeks and froze. I watched it until the howling wind drove me back under the snow.

On the fourth day I fell down and when I tried to get up I could not. I closed my eyes and lay still. I would have slept if it had not been for the wracking cough. It seemed to start somewhere back in my throat and then lance all the way down to my belly, shredding my lungs in the process.

"Get up, dawg," Wilder called.

"I can't," I said, without moving.

"Get the fuck up," Wilder said.

I turned my face out of the snow and said: "I can't. Fuck it. I ca-" and then I started to cough.

"Hey Doc," Muddy said, "come on man. Get up. We got to keep moving."

I looked at Muddy. I knew there was a little blood smeared around my mouth. I shook my head. "I can't," I said. "I feel like something broke. I can't do it. Just go."

Wilder and Muddy exchanged glances. They left for a moment and I thought they were leaving but they stopped walking and started whispering. I only heard Muddy say one thing, in a soft urgent tone: "...still six days till we get to Rocky Bay, and we don't even know..."

Wilder muttered something in response that I couldn't understand because of his accent.

"Okay, let me try again," Muddy said.

"Nah," Wilder said in his normal tone, "I'll do it."

I felt him troop back over to me. "What the fuck Doc?" he said. "What the fuck? You goan to give up like this?"

"I can't."

"The fuck you can't!" he shouted. "You're letting them win. You dig me? This what they want. They want you to die. You just goan to lie there and do it?"

I didn't care anymore. That didn't work on me.

Wilder leaned down and seized my hair. "For what? What was it all for? Why was you even born? Why'd you fight? Why'd you do all the things you did? To do this?"

I closed my eyes.

"So that's it then? You ain't got nothing? You can't think of one reason, on your own self, to get the fuck up right now?"

I thought. And I thought, for a moment, of my tie rack. The little buzzing noise the motor made as it moved my ties around. I remembered that, and then I remembered how my wife complained about it, how she said she didn't know why I needed so many ties when I didn't have to wear them to work. And then I remembered my wife, and our coffee machine, and my car, and my patients and the hockey team my office sponsored. But I also knew, intellectually, that those days were gone and would never come back. So I didn't feel any hope. I just remembered a time before I was a concentration camp prisoner, starved to the bone, stripped of all his morals, joyless and hollow. And I felt a little pride.

"Help me up," I said.

It wasn't so bad when I was on my feet. I walked a few yards, carefully, so I didn't crack the ice. Then I said: "Thanks guys. Thanks a lot."

Wilder grinned at me, but for some reason, Muddy wouldn't look me in the eyes.

*****

Of the three of us, it was Muddy who had the easiest time walking on the snow. I was sick and weak, while Wilder was blundering and heavy. But Muddy was as graceful as a daddy longlegs and he'd frequently have to wait for us, standing on the snow as easily as if it were cement. That's why it was so surprising when he broke his ankle.

It was two days after I had collapsed and we were completely out of food. We were exactly at the limit of human endurance. The hunger was so paralyzing I wasn't sure I'd be able to get up and walk the next day. I knew that within a little while we would be dead.

We were on one of the islands, just a little square of rock a few feet above the frozen lake. One or two tall pines rose above our head. Wilder was preparing our shelter for the evening with my ineffectual help. Muddy gathering branches for a fire, although I wasn't sure why we needed one. It was always unpleasantly warm in the shelter anyway.

I happened to be watching Muddy when his foot suddenly plunged through the snow and an expression of pain exploded across his face.

I was on my feet immediately and rushed over to him. "What's wrong?" I asked. "Are you okay?"

Muddy was lying on his side. His leg came out of the snow and I could see that his foot was bent at an unnatural angle.

"Oh my god," I said, and shuffled over as quickly as I could. "Don't try to move!"

"I'm fine!" Muddy barked. He hid his broken ankle behind his body and looked at me with something like pure hatred. I stopped in my tracks.

"I'm fine, leave me alone," he repeated.

"Let me see it," I said. "I got a lot of practice setting broken bones in the infirmary."

"It's not broken!" Muddy cried. His eyes were wide and wild, and you could still read his pain in the lines etched around his face. "I said I'm fucking fine, all right? Mind your own business."

And then he looked past me and though he tried to hide it, I could see that he was afraid.

"What's the matter?" I asked.

"Nothing's the matter, I just slipped all right?" Muddy seemed on the verge of tears. "Why won't you just fuck off? Okay? Just fuck off! I'm fine."

"What are you worried about?" I said. "There's nothing to be afraid of."

And then Muddy started to laugh. He didn't look at me. Instead he stared down into the snow and he laughed, and the sound of it was very, very bitter. After a while he trailed off and his shoulders started heaving like he was about to cry but when he spoke his voice was firm: "You stupid, stupid son of a bitch. Oh my God."

"Stand up Muddy," Wilder said from behind me. I turned to look at him. His face was impassive.

"In a minute," Muddy said.

"I think you better stand up right now," Wilder said.

"He can't stand," I said, "his ankle's broken. I saw it."

"Oh will you shut up?" Muddy said.

Now he looked at Wilder and his upper lip peeled back from his teeth.

"You stay the fuck away from me, Wilder," he said, and pulled his knife from his belt.

"Whoa!" I said. I stuck my arm out across Wilder's chest to hold him back. "What's going ..."

Wilder hit me hard in the temple, stunning me, and sending me stumbling to the snow. A moment later I heard Muddy scream and then fall silent. When I got up on my knees, I saw Muddy on his back, blood pumping out of his neck in regular arterial spurts, and Wilder wiping the blade on his pants.

"Oh my god," I said, and scrambled over towards Muddy. Wilder looked at me and I froze.

It took Muddy a long time to die. He looked from me to Wilder and then back to me again, over and over. Finally he looked into the sunset, back the way we'd come, and he was still.

"What the fuck?" I finally said. "Why did you do that?"

"Had to," Wilder said.

"You dumb fucking murderer!" I screamed. "You didn't have to! We could have helped him! We were a team!"

Wilder threw back his head and laughed.

"Don't you fucking laugh at me!" I said. "You didn't even give him a chance. He might not have slowed us down – anyway, we didn't have to kill him!"

"*Slow us down*? Dawg, that ain't it. We gotta *eat*."

There was a moment of silence, the kind so pure you can only find it in the middle of a frozen lake three hundred miles from anything.

"What do you mean, we gotta eat?" I said stupidly. "You're going to eat Muddy?"

Wilder watched me, his ropey dreadlocks hanging around his bearded mouth.

"We gotta eat," he said, his voice flat and declaratory. "It's four days to Rocky Bay, and there might not even be anybody there. If we don't eat him, we ain't going to make it.

The wheels were slowly turning in my mind.

He looked at me, still grinning, showing those yellow crooked teeth, and I didn't ask what we would have done if Muddy hadn't hurt himself.

Because suddenly I knew.

*****

Wilder stripped the corpse where it lay in the blood soaked snow and then he took the knife to it. Muddy's brown body, emaciated from months of malnutrition, yielded a surprising amount of meat. Soon everything was coated in red. Wilder ran the knife down through the thighs, cutting what flesh there was off the bones. The calves came next, then the triceps and biceps and buttocks. Snow white fat, flopping tendons, exposed bone. Hair and blood and ropes of slimy intestine.

At first I couldn't watch. Then I couldn't look away. Then I walked away, in the dark, with the moon hanging over head, heading nowhere in particular. After a while I heard Wilder call out.

"Doc! Get back here!"

I turned and looked at him, standing on the island, around a hundred metres away.

"I'm a follow your footsteps, Doc! You get your ass back here!"

I walked back, wearily, and sat down next to Wilder. It was getting very cold. My lips, nose and cheeks were screaming in pain. Up above the moon had set and the stars were burning like the tiny suns they were. The constellations were all so vivid and clear.

"Start the fire," Wilder said.

I took the wood Muddy had gathered and crawled into the shelter and used his lighter to set some paper alight. The small branches caught, and then the bigger ones. I fed the fire green sticks, one after another, until it was strong enough to burn some thicker branches from a dead tree. The shelter had a crude chimney but the little igloo still filled with smoke and I started to cough. I lay on the floor where the air was clear.

A moment later Wilder came inside with the meat and a flat rock. He was comically hunched inside the igloo. If he stood up he'd have broken through the ceiling, which was already melting dangerously around the chimney. He put the stone in the fire and then laid some rough strips of red flesh on the stone.

I slept, only to be awoken by the smell of cooking meat.

There are three salivary glands in the human mouth. One is behind the front teeth on the bottom of the mouth, and the other two are next to the molars on either side of the mouth. The production of saliva is an involuntary reaction. You have to understand, I had not eaten in days. Have you ever, dear reader, gone a single day without food? Do you know what it is to walk miles and miles in the frozen north, your body frantically burning energy to keep you warm, ploughing through snow deeper than you can stand? The body simply takes over. It pushes the mind away and gets into the driver's seat.

I stared at that meat, watched it sizzle on the rock. The smoke of it getting into my nose. Slobber running out of the cracked and bleeding corners of my mouth. I tried to say something but could not.

Wilder watched the meat too, for what seemed like hours. Then he deftly picked it up and tossed it in the snow, next to me.

I looked at the strip of Muddy's flesh, and it helped (a little) that it was disgusting. Grey and stringy and burned at little bit from the heat. I tossed it away.

"No," he said. "Eat it."

"No," I said.

"Eat it, bro. You need your strength, you going to make it to Rocky Bay."

"Forget it," I said. "I'm not going to make it to Rocky Bay. Go ahead and kill me if you like."

"I don't want to carry your carcass all the way there," Wilder said. "Better if you walk. But I will if I gotta."

I shrugged.

Wilder picked up the meat and put it in his mouth and bit into it. It was so tough he almost pulled his teeth loose trying to rip it apart. Instead he chewed it slowly and patiently.

"Who you trying to impress?" he said. "Ain't no one else out here."

I said nothing.

"He was going to eat you. Me and him planned it. Walk you halfway across the lake then eat you and make it the rest of the way."

I said nothing.

"You'll eat," he said. "You can't hold out."

"You don't get it," I said finally. "If they do this to us, they win."

"Who?"

"Them," I said. "If we ... if we give up everything we believe in, if we just put preserving our own lives above everything else, then they win. Because they've stripped everything good away from us. I won't let them take that from me. I'd rather die. Life isn't worth anything when all the rest is gone."

Wilder looked at me, his murderous eyes dancing with silent laughter.

"They win? Shit, doc. Why'd you think they sent us all up to this camp? To make us bad? To take something? Shit. They sent us to die. That's all. It don't matter if you die the hero or the villain. It don't matter if you die doing every last thing they say like a bitch, if you die sticking it to 'em like a hero, if you die for being a righteous man, like you got a mind to. If you die, you giving 'em exactly what they after. You wanna stick it to them? Don't die. That's all."

Was it true? Was the only way to truly resist a system engineered to cause one's own death to live, no matter what the cost? To keep breathing, to see another sunset? To refuse to be tossed into the dustbin of history with the faceless hordes? Did it really not matter, who kept themselves and who sold?

Another piece of burnt flesh landed next to me and I took it in my hands and put it in my mouth. I made no conscious decision. My body reacted like a drowning man grasping at a rope.

Wilder watched me and smiled.

*****

Four days later we came to the edge of the lake. The trees on the shoreline formed a dark line against the horizon. I had no idea whether we would be able to find Rocky Bay, which was a tiny Indian reserve tucked away in the southeast corner of the lake.

When we hit the shore we cut south, where the lake cut a path through the trees about a kilometre wide. We came to the docks just as the sun was setting behind us and climbed back up onto solid land. It was immediately apparent the town was abandoned.

"Aw fuck no," Wilder said. "Fuck this shit."

Two streets ran parallel north and south, and another cut across them and headed off, presumably to the main highway. The snow was piled up high; no one had ploughed it all year. The sad little houses for the Indians, cheap beige shanty bungalows, built all close, like barracks, were all empty. We kicked in the doors to one or two of them and didn't find a thing to eat anywhere. The cupboards were all completely bare and the fridges were dark and smelled foul. There weren't even any rats.

We stood in one kitchen, Wilder and I, the wallpaper peeling, cheap linoleum beneath our feet. I was exhausted and my stomach was screaming in agony. I looked at him and asked if he was going to kill me.

He just shook his head.

"You're getting attached to me," I said.

"Nah dawg," he said. "We be all right. We'll get out on the road tomorrow."

Neither he nor I bothered to say the obvious; that it could easily be a hundred kilometres to the next town or service station.

We sat down on the floor for the night. It was actually colder than it had been in the shelters and I found it difficult to sleep. My stomach felt shrivelled and every time I started to drop off I would suddenly jerk awake, afraid to see Wilder leaning over me with the knife.

Eventually I sat up and looked at the ceiling. I smiled. I don't know why; I hadn't smiled in days and the cracks in my lips and the corners of my mouth split open and started to bleed. I was going to die. It wasn't so bad. I had given everything. I could honestly say that. I was exhausted and starving, sick and tired and cold. There was nothing left. I could die without a shred of regret.

Wilder sat up too. I realized he hadn't been sleeping. Perhaps he had been worried about me running off, or trying to kill him.

"Can't sleep, doc?"

I shrugged. So dark we could barely see each other.

"This ain't like being a dentist, is it?"

"No, not like that," I said.

"I ain't never been to the dentist."

"I hope you brushed," I said. Then: "Flossed too."

"I bet that's a good job," Wilder said.

"I loved being a dentist. But a lot of guys don't like it."

"Why not?"

"I don't know," I said. "It just happens a lot with professionals. Doctors, dentists, accountants, lawyers. Sometimes people when they're young, they aren't sure what they want to do. Being a professional is easy if you're smart, you just stay in school and then go out and practice. A lot of people, when they finally start, they're disappointed. The work can be a little boring, frankly, not very stimulating, kind of repetitive. They're expecting something more but they sort of get stuck. They only know how to do one thing, they feel like it's too late to do something else, or they can't afford to, because they have to make payments on their house or send their kids to private school. And so they go to work every day, miserable."

I smiled again at this, so the blood ran down my chin at a pretty steady trickle. Miserable, going to the office. Everything in life is relative.

I wondered how much Wilder understood of what I'd just said, but then he said: "Some folks don't appreciate what they got."

"There was a friend of mine," I said. "Partner, really. We shared an office. He hated his life. Always used to complain. Always used to tell young people not to go to dental school, and so on. I just sort of listened. One time I tried to help. I asked him, if he didn't like it, why didn't he quit? He said he couldn't. I said, sure he could. Just quit. Do something else. He said he needed the money for his kids. I said, well, you can quit, kids or no. So if you don't, you're choosing to come in every day. You're saying, I will go into this job, this job I don't like. You make that choice. Why? For your kids. So every time you do a filling, you look at an x-ray, you crown a tooth or cover up a sensitive root, you aren't doing it because you're being forced to. You're choosing to do it for them. I told him that all of his boredom and frustration had a purpose. I said, David, that was his name, David, I said, David: you're doing the noblest thing anyone can do. You're sacrificing yourself for love, every day. It's the most amazing thing in the world."

It was quiet for a while and I felt myself drifting into a kind of sleep. Then Wilder suddenly spoke:

"Did it help?"

And I laughed, I couldn't help it. "Oh Wilder," I finally said, "no, of course not Wilder. Of course it didn't help."

*****

We left Rocky Bay well before dawn and trudged northeast in the dark along the unploughed road that led (presumably) to the highway. In less than an hour we arrived at a service station.

I realized then that until that moment I had never experienced unalloyed happiness. Always before, anything good had been tainted by some minor disappointment, or inseparably entangled with the perception of some flaw. A victory in jiu-jitsu, my graduation from dental school, the sight of my wife's naked body. Always that little carping voice, that critical eye.

But now, as I stumbled out of the snow onto the ploughed road, feeling the healthy click of frozen gravel under my heels, and that beautiful rural gas station and restaurant ("The Friendly Restaurant" was printed on its roof in bright red letters), I had an entirely pure moment of unbelieving ecstasy.

Wilder and I stumbled past the rusting pumps to the window of the restaurant. It was brightly lit, with a chrome counter and tables with plastic table cloths and booths with red vinyl seating. A middle-aged man was behind the counter fiddling with the coffee machines. Coffee! Drool squirted out the corners of my mouth and froze on my face.

"Go in the front," Wilder said. "I'm a go 'round the back."

"What?"

"You go in," he said. "Don't let him call the cops."

And then I realized; we were fugitives from justice, completely penniless.

"Okay," I said.

A chime sounded as I opened the door, and oh god all mighty, I stepped into a heated room. The warmth settled over me like a blanket, not getting all the way inside yet, but starting to work its way in. I couldn't smell any food but I could see pies and pastries underneath the glass counter and I started drooling again.

The man behind the counter stared at me.

I smiled in what, in my imagination, was a comforting fashion.

"Who the hell are you?" the man said. "Where did you come from?"

"Car broke down," I said. "Man, am I glad to see you."

I started walking forward. Unaccountably, the man was violently afraid.

"You can't come in here!" he said.

"What do you mean? It's freezing outside."

The man was genuinely terrified. I could see it in his eyes. He ducked under the counter and came up with a shotgun.

"Get the fuck outside!" he said in a wavering voice.

"Whoa! Whoa!" I said. "I'm cold and I need a place to rest! I'm not going to hurt you!"

"Get out or I'll shoot!" he said. "And then I'm going to call the cops!"

"What the fuck man," I cried out, with what was entirely sincere indignation. But then Wilder stepped out of the kitchen, looming over the counterman, and I realized that his fear had been completely, one hundred percent justified. That he had seen me for exactly what I was – a criminal, a fugitive from justice, a man who planned to murder him. That this man, who had only seen me for a brief second, knew me better in this moment than I knew myself.

My eyes must have flicked over to Wilder and the counterman tried to wheel around but it was too late. Wilder caught the barrel of the shotgun and wrested it away and threw the counterman on the ground who screamed for help.

I turned around and locked the door to the diner and then I started pulling down the blinds. Behind me the counterman fell silent. By the time I finished Wilder was already pulling out a half-eaten lemon meringue pie from underneath the counter. He ripped off the saran wrap from it and started shovelling it down with bloodstained hands.

I started whimpering as I ran over. I vaulted over the counter and scrambled with the counter's sliding door and managed to produce a handful of stale doughnuts which I crammed into my mouth. Beside me I could hear Wilder struggling not to throw up, which should have made me slow down, but did not. I almost choked myself, and then afterwards the food sat in my stomach like a painful stone.

After a moment the frenzy passed I stood up and looked around for some orange juice. There was a jug in the fridge and I tilted it up to my mouth and drank. That went down much easier. I felt like I could feel my body starting to start up again and work, to come back to life.

Wilder staggered into the kitchen after me and fired up the griddle. He splashed oil over it and cracked egg after egg down where they started to spit and sizzle. Then he threw down two fistfuls of bacon. The smell grew powerful and I thought I might be sick so I wandered back into the restaurant with the jug of orange juice in my hand and I almost tripped over the corpse of the counterman.

I looked down. His head had been smashed open with the butt of his own shotgun and an enormous pool of blood had spread over the tiled floor. Now it was growing tacky and thick. I looked at him, and I thought, I had to kill him. I had to kill him in the most very real sense. If I had not killed him, I would have died. But in my heart I knew this was not a bad man, and he had not done anything to me. I had chosen to end his life rather than to die myself.

I saw my reflection in the chrome. Small wonder the counterman had been frightened of me. It wasn't just my emaciated face, the beard, the dirt, the bits of human flesh caught between my teeth. It was the eyes. There was something different about my eyes. I leaned in closer and stared into them, but for the life of me, I couldn't quite figure out what it was.

Somewhere along the line, I'm not exactly sure when, I decided to survive. Did that make me a hero or a villain? To refuse to die? To make other people die instead of me, so I could keep living? Was that resistance or not? Was it resistance to stay yourself and die and vanish so utterly that it was as if you never were? Or was it resistance to fight and claw and kill others, so that you became a part of the horror yourself? For this dead man, his story was over, while mine would go on. I was to him what the camp was to me.

Perhaps resistance was impossible; perhaps heroism was a dream. Perhaps none of us were free. One thing alone was impossible to deny; that I felt more alive in those moments, with death at my heels, than I had done in years. I felt as if I had run some terrible gauntlet and come out into a new place, where each thing was a miracle, a repository of light-headed joy.

I walked around the counter and sat down in one of the booths and took a long, sweet drink of orange juice. The smell of eggs and bacon hung in the air. I leaned back into the seat and closed my eyes and felt the heat of the diner seep into my bones.

*****

Wilder is shouting at me from downstairs. One more thing, then, before I go.

I said before I have no children, and this is true, but I had a very close relationship with my cousin's son, a boy named Danilo. This cousin was the daughter of my mother's younger brother. She was a bit of a skid and Danilo grew up without a father. He was fourteen years younger than me and I'd always tried to take the time to help him out, especially after I got a job and I could afford to buy him things.

But Danilo was enormously troubled and he ended up taking his own life about three years ago. They buried him in his Leafs jersey in a ceremony attended by all of his high school friends where I sat so grief-stricken and wounded that I knew that on some level I would never be whole again.

They say the ones that talk about doing it are never the ones that actually do it, kill yourself, I mean, but I can tell you that's total bullshit. We all saw it coming with Danilo, like a car crash in slow motion, but there was just nothing we could do.

You can send people to therapy and you can pump them full of drugs and you can keep telling them it's okay, that they're all right, that everyone likes them, but none of it gets all the way down, do you see, all the way down to where people really are. In the end everyone is alone and life is hard and you have to stand or fall all by yourself.

I remember towards the end I was in his room talking to him. We were making plans about what we were going to do every day next week. Seeing movies or playing sports or something and he seemed fine, he seemed as if he was doing okay, when all of a sudden he started to cry. And so we sat there, for a little while, and he cried and I looked away. And in that moment I knew that he was going to die.

Danilo slowly got himself under control. He wiped his eyes and sniffled and looked at me and suddenly he smiled, in the kind of way that could break your heart. And he asked me: *Do you know why everyone is so depressed these days, even though we all have everything we could ever want?* And I said, no, Danilo, I honestly don't. And he kept smiling even though he was starting to cry again, and he said: "Because there's nothing to worry about."

4 Natural and Unnatural Animals

*I never saw a wild thing
sorry for itself.
A small bird will drop frozen dead from a bough
without ever having felt sorry for itself.*

D.H. Lawrence

Two farmhouses. One, at the bottom of a steep slope, was owned by a lonely, vicious man named Tony Baldwell. A little while before this story begins his timid wife had finally scooped up their soft little bruised children and driven off to parts unknown. Tony never saw them again, despite his drunken late-night calls to his wife's friends and relatives.

Tony had a big blue truck and a few acres and a stupid, loud mongrel dog named Max. A herd of cows and a couple of mud-splattered horses wandered aimlessly in the poorly fenced paddock behind his faded and peeling bungalow. A sharp, steep slope rose past the paddock, and at the top of the hill there was another farmhouse.

The second house was owned by the Johnson family. They were a nice couple, somewhat past middle age, who had purchased a farm after their children had moved out and gone to college. They had made friends with Mrs. Baldwell before her daring escape, and occasionally Tony would phone them up past midnight and scream terrible curses at them that would make the quiet, urbane Johnsons quake with fear.

Matthew Johnson was a lawyer in Toronto. He had come to loathe his job, but it would be some time before he could retire because he needed to pay off his new mortgage and help his three children finish university. Matt was tall and stooping and he had always wanted to live in the country. His wife Pam was brown and talked loud and always smiled. She was quite pretty although she was getting on in years and she loved Matt very much because she had been quite poor as a child and she took great satisfaction in the affluent lifestyle that her husband had worked so hard for.

They had brought a dog with them to their new home; a purebred golden retriever bitch they called Maggie. And it was not long before they acquired a stray cat. Pam found the little creature shuddering in the rain, emaciated and frightened, and brought it inside. It took them a while to name the cat, who was elderly and ragged around the edges and had a nasty cough. For a long time the Johnsons simply called it the cat. Eventually they settled on Felix, because Felix is Latin for "lucky" and as Pam said, Felix was certainly a lucky cat. Her coat was smoothening out and she lay for hours in the sun and her only occupation was hunting mice. Much better than shivering all alone out in the cold.

To a human, the cat is a funny little creature, not quite wild like a fox but not really tame like a dog. It has an endearing little cry and claws and teeth which are more amusing than dangerous. It is a little creature you point at when it is lying asleep and you are working and you say wouldn't that be nice, a little creature that purrs when you pet it, a little creature that exists around the periphery of your existence and you don't really think about very much at all.

To the mice scattered through the little house (which had been pretty rundown before the Johnsons bought it; it was a 'fixer-upper') Felix appeared somewhat differently. To them, Felix was a towering, sadistic tormentor. To them, Felix was as swift and as silent and as merciless and as beautiful as death herself. To them, Felix was not an amusing diversion that could be carelessly pushed aside but an unappeasable force that sought only their destruction.

And then Felix grew heavy, and round.

*****

Animals do not have names. They speak their own private language which we humans once knew but have now forgotten in favor of our own tongues, which are nicer but contain great gaps for which no word exists. The speech of the beasts of the field is not so fine but it contains everything in the universe.

The mouse I shall call John was born in a nest of shredded paper and insulation between the ceiling of the basement and the floor of the kitchen in the Johnson home while Felix silently paced above him. John began life not much different than a worm; pink and hairless with bulging blue eyes that were shut fast, mewling quietly, unable to move. He had seven brothers and sisters. He never knew his father, for shortly after John's conception his father fell to Felix.

John grew quickly, which is the nature of mice, but in many ways he was unlike his fellows. He was smaller than normal, for instance, and there were white rings around his eyes. His mother said that they must make him blind, for

John lacked the deep, instinctual fears that a mouse needs to stay alive. He rarely hugged close to walls and corners, preferring instead to amble through open spaces. And he was very curious and thoughtful, unusual characteristics for a mouse. John would often spend a long time looking at things and thinking about them in a highly unnatural manner.

His mother and his brethren despaired for John's survival, but he outlived almost all of them. Felix claimed John's mother when he was around a half-year old. They had been scurrying back from a sack of grain in the corner of the cellar to their little hole when the cat had silently fallen among them like the wrath of god. The terrible shrieks of John's mother followed him as he bolted like lightning to the hole and dived for cover. But then, unlike his cowering brothers and sisters and aunts and uncles, John poked his head back out of the mouse-hole to watch the final moments of the creature who had given him life.

She was dazed and bleeding and so frightened that she could barely move. Her flanks were rising and falling so rapidly that it was a wonder her heart did not simply burst from the exertion. Felix was hunched over her front paws with her tail swishing high in the air above her head. Occasionally she would extend a paw and bat her tiny victim off of her feet. Whenever John's mother tried to flee, Felix would pounce and catch her between her jaws and squeeze while the little mouse squeaked with terror. Eventually the cat tired of the game and so she ended it. As Felix padded silently towards the stairs, the limp mouse dangling from its fangs, John heard himself screaming.

You monster!

John, the other mice whimpered from behind him, *stop it, come back with us! What are you doing, you unnatural mouse!*

You monster! John cried out in the common patois of the animals in his reedy rodent voice.

Felix turned her head, and the dead mouse's tail and hind legs swished in the air below her jaw. The cat's weird flat eyes seemed to glow in the darkness while it pupils expanded to see in the dark. She spat out the body of the mouse and quickly trotted over towards the hole. John tried to stand his ground, and he did for a little while, but then the call of instinct was too strong and he found himself pushed against his will into the safety of the hole.

An unnatural mouse, Felix said, in a voice halfway between a purr and a hiss. *A little unnatural mouse. Well well well. Come out, little mouse, and let us speak some more.*

John said nothing. He trembled with fear and hatred and grief.

The cat pressed its face up against the hole and the mice looked into her glowing eyes and shuddered.

Come on, mouse. Attack me. Perhaps I shall choke on your bones.

You're a monster! John shouted again, though he did not move.

It is my nature to eat mice. Would you have me starve, little mouse?

You didn't have to torture her!

Ah, said the cat. *I suppose I didn't. But that too is my nature. That is the order of all things. It is you, little one, who is the monster, not I. It is you who does not belong.*

No! John said. *I don't hurt anyone! You cats are the ones who hurt! I hate you all!*

Hate? the cat said, amused. *I perform my role. You perform yours. We are not enemies. We are dance partners. So come out, little unnatural mouse. And let us dance.*

John said no more. The cat chuckled and wandered off and picked up the dead mouse. She carried it up to the bedroom. The Johnsons had just finished making love.

"Oh shit."

"Ugh, Felix! Bad cat! Don't bring that here!"

"Meow!" Felix said.

"We have to do something about the mice around here," Matt said.

"Poor little mouse," said Pat, looking at the tiny corpse.

"Meow!" Felix said.

The other mice shivered and endured and forgot. But John remembered and vowed revenge.

*****

When the kittens were born the mice were struck dumb with fear. One cat was bad enough, and now there were five more? The mice thought back wistfully to the tales of their grandfathers, who spoke of the days before there were cats, and the mice had only needed to avoid the traps of men.

It is the nature of mice to endure, not to seek to alter their world. But John, who was swiftly gaining a reputation as a terribly unnatural mouse, had a different idea. He crouched for hours in the tunnels that riddled the Johnson home, desperately trying to make the connections that were flickering like live wires in his head.

His thoughts kept returning to the big yellow dog. John thought of the dog, and he thought of the cat, and he thought of the kittens.

Then his mind slipped back to mouse thoughts, to the here and now, and he thought of breeding and eating and keeping hidden and what he should be doing this very moment. But through force of will he turned his mind back to the dog and he thought to himself the dog, the dog could kill the cats if only it could be persuaded.

Finally John summoned his courage and slipped out of the mice tunnels around noon, when the yellow dog was usually asleep in the shade under the porch. John left the house through a tear in the screen door and looked down through the cracks of the deck at the massive form of the sleeping dog.

Every instinct told him to run silently back to safety, but John's flickering conscious mind fought his mouse-mind as well as it could and the end result was that his muscles froze up like rusty gears and he couldn't have moved to save his life.

Eventually, he forced himself to cry out: *Dog!*

Maggie was not sleeping, only lying peacefully. She looked up and saw the mouse peeking at it through the porch.

Hey! Maggie yelled. *Hey! Hey! Heyyyyyyyy! What are you doing, you mouse? Hey hey hey!*

"Shut up Maggie!" Matt yelled from inside the house.

Shh, quiet dog! John said.

This is my house! Maggie said in a calmer voice. She loved Pam but feared Matt and always made sure to be quiet when he told her to. *Get off my porch! Filthy mouse! Hey!*

Shh, dog, listen to me!

Maggie began to pant. *What do you want, and then go away.*

Dog, I need you to kill the cat.

What!

"Maggie! Shut up!"

I'm not going to kill Felix, you dirty little mouse! She's my mommy!

This was beyond John's limited comprehension. He tried again, saying *Dog, if you kill the cat, then the house will be ours. Eat the little kittens! Then we can have this house for mice and dogs only. After all, there is no quarrel between us and...*

Sss!

John jumped and turned around. A garden snake, green and yellow and all shifting scales was twining its way along the deck. John's muscles moved without consulting his brain and in a flash John was back in the house and in the tunnels, his heart beating wildly and his conscious mind shattered into a thousand pieces like glass.

A little while later Felix wandered outside, awakened by the barking, and saw the snake slithering across the deck. She crouched and flicked her tail and remained perfectly motionless as it slowly passed by. Then she stood up and stretched casually and wandered under the deck to meet Maggie.

The young dog barked affectionately and jumped from side to side sniffing the little cat who carefully rubbed the side of her face on the dog's flank, marking it as her property.

I saw a filthy little mouse today Mom, Maggie said.

Did you now, precious?

Yes, it wanted me to eat your babies. Filthy mouse. Hey!"

The cat froze. She had thought herself infertile and the kittens had come very late in life.

Little unnatural mouse, the cat whispered. *They are dangerous, the unnatural animals.*

The dog licked her.

But then, the cat reflected, it is only a mouse. And soon my children, my replacements, my immortality will be strong hunters in their own right. And we will purge this house of the mice as tribute to the humans. And I shall never truly die for my seed will be transmitted forever throughout time in cats like myself, an unbroken ribbon through eternity.

*****

The kittens were growing older. They were still drinking their mother's milk but now they could blunder around the little room where Felix kept her nest. John would watch them surreptitiously from time to time. There was a small hole behind the sugar jar on the counter and John could look down on the young monsters from above, shuddering with fear, his instincts telling him to run but his fledgling conscious mind telling him to stay.

There had to be a way to kill the kittens before they grew older. There was some sort of way. It flickered on and off in his mind like an elderly light bulb but it never seemed to fully catch.

John had his revelation one day when he was scurrying through the shadows where the wall met the floor in the living room. The floor suddenly began to shake with Matt's heavy footsteps and John quickly scurried under a chair.

Matt walked into the room and cried out in disgust when he saw the little droppings that John had left on the floor.

"Goddamn it!"

"What's the matter, baby?" Pam called from upstairs.

"More mouse shit."

"Oh."

"We need to get an exterminator out here," Matt said. He was so busy with his job in the city paying for his place that he didn't have the time to take care of it properly and he found it profoundly frustrating.

John stayed under the couch while Matt walked out of the room briefly and then came back holding a thin green tube in his hand. He shook the tube in the corner of the room, where the mice had gnawed a small hole.

"Are you sure the cats won't eat that?" Pam asked as she wandered down into the room.

Matt grumbled something that sounded suspiciously like "no." He straightened and put a hand on his back. Pam gave him a quick peck on the cheek. When they left the room John scurried out from under the chair and ran over to the hole where Matt had been shaking the tube. The ground was littered with small whitish pellets. John stopped and stared at them. He was right in the middle of the floor, completely exposed, and every instinct in his body told him to run for cover. But he was thinking, thinking.

Those pellets. John knew them well. They smelled like food but if you bit into them you would get terrible pains in your stomach and then die. When John had left this hole, they hadn't been here. Now they had appeared.

Before they hadn't been there ... now they were.

John thought and thought and thought.

Did the pellets come because the human had shook the tube? Were they somehow ... inside the tube? Like the mice were inside the walls?

John realized he had seen the green tube before. It sat on the corner of the kitchen counter, high above the nest of the cats.

Could the pellets kill kittens as well as mice?

Troubled with thoughts such as these, John retreated back into the tunnels that riddled the Johnson home.

*****

A few days later, one of the kittens leapt out from underneath a sofa and pounced on John. It only batted him back and forth for a while, watching him curiously and jumping around playfully, but it frightened John so badly that he thought his poor heart would split in half. Eventually he escaped into the walls and swore that he would try to poison the kittens that night.

And so it was that John found himself scurrying along the edge of the kitchen counter in the dead of the night, skipping nimbly between the dark and cold stove elements and weaving in between the jars of spices until he came to the edge overlooking the cats.

John peered down and saw them. The five little kittens were tangled together lying on a woolen blanket. Not far from them was a shallow saucer of milk. Felix was nowhere to be seen.

John retreated back from the edge. The green tube was standing up next to him, tall and mysterious and reeking of death.

And suddenly he didn't know what to do. The pictures simply wouldn't form in his little mouse mind. There was something … the tube … the kittens … the milk. What could he do?

It was a maddening sensation, but the more John tried to think it through, the more frightened and worried he became, the more he glanced around nervously for the approaching form of Felix, the more his mind spluttered and splintered and refused to make the pictures.

Finally, more out of desperation than anything else, John hurled his little body against the green tube. It toppled over and fell on its side, and a large number of pellets tumbled out the top and streamed over the counter.

The kittens awoke and pounced to and fro in the darkness. John turned and ran back to his hole, cursing himself, thinking he had failed.

Before the kittens went back to sleep they drank from the saucer.

*****

Now that Felix's children were old enough to move about on their own, she found herself needing more and more time away from them. The kittens had an endless supply of energy and they could be quite exhausting. Felix would slip away to hidden places outside the house for a few short hours to recuperate her strength.

She returned late at night and found one of her children retching on the linoleum floor. The other four were dead.

Felix's first reaction was panic. She began yowling in terror and moving the bodies of the kittens around with her paws and licking them all over. When the last one grew quiet and still she ran around in a frantic circle as if chasing her own tail and then bolted up the stairs and leapt up onto Matt and Pam's bed and meowed frantically and ran all over them. Matt only cursed and chased her away.

Back over the children once again, Felix glanced over to the saucer and finally noticed the strange odor of the milk. She paused. And then the wheels in her mind very slowly began to turn.

With one smooth movement she leapt up onto the counter that was an infinite height to a mouse. And what she saw first was not the toppled bottle nor the tiny pellets of poison but instead a single, lonely mouse dropping.

At first, Felix's rage was terrible, verging on madness, but not especially dangerous. She hurled herself at the holes in the walls, spitting and yowling and screeching until Matt came downstairs and was stunned into silence by the sight of the dead kittens.

Mouse! Felix screamed. *Unnatural mouse! I'll kill you! Kill you! Kill! I'll get you, mouse! Mouse!* She reached into the holes with one of her lean arms and extended her claws and flailed around wildly.

Inside, the mice cowered. John's courage was gone. The wrath of the cat was so awesome that it was impossible for him to remember the past or imagine the future. He could only stare in bewildered horror at the present moment.

Matt and Pam buried the little kittens in the backyard but Felix would not allow herself to be stroked or comforted or even touched.

When Felix's rage slipped from murderous fury to a more calculating passion for revenge, she became very dangerous.   Before Felix had been a menace, but an inconsistent one. Some days she would hunt, but others she would allow the mice to scamper right past her unmolested. And she would only kill to satiate her hunger or to amuse herself in quiet moments.

But now Felix became dedicated to killing every last mouse in the Johnson home. She rarely slept, and only stalked about the periphery of the walls, watching the main mouse-holes from the shadows. Whenever she saw a mouse she would pounce on it and kill it instantly, moving on to the next one like a bolt of lightning. The numbers of mice began to dwindle rapidly.

But Felix could not find John. He grew gaunt and thin, but he subsisted on scraps and rarely left the security of the walls. She would forget, John thought.

It is not the nature of animals to bear grudges. No natural animal would remember the death of its young for so long. How could you? You would go mad, remembering such tragedies. Mad like the humans who sought to destroy the whole world. But Felix must have been a fairly unnatural animal herself, for she remembered. Long after the mice (save John) had forgotten the cause of her rage, it continued unabated.

Finally, the mice called a meeting in a small, dark hollowed space in a nest of ripped paper and insulation.

We must leave, said John.

We cannot, an older mouse said. *Where would we go? We cannot survive in the wilderness. The beasts are too great and many. They would make our current tormentor seem as a child. We must endure.*

Our numbers dwindle, John said. *We cannot last much longer. We have lost too many women. Last week, Felix took Nancy when she was heavy with child. The rest of us are growing old. There is less and less to eat on the inside. When we begin to venture out we will be weak and helpless. We must move the whole colony away from the cat.*

But where?

I have a plan, said John. *Do you remember the rats?*

Rats, rats, the mice whispered, in fear and in awe.

*****

Rats are similar enough to mice to have a shared understanding, but the rats far exceed their smaller cousins in size, intelligence, and courage. The mice venerate the rats as creatures higher than themselves, worthy of respect but also dangerous and wild. To rats, mice are nothing but cowardly vermin, but there is enough fellow feeling between the two races to ensure that the rats are usually kind to mice.

There was a large and particularly cunning colony of rats down at the base of the hill, in Tony's run-down old home. They lived in a network of tunnels beneath the cellars and fed on whatever they could steal. They were bold enough to eat directly from Max's bowl and since Tony was not a cleanly man now that his wife had left, the rats fed like kings on mostly-empty jars of cheese whiz, discarded pizza boxes and other bits of this and that.

The rats' warren was under the domination of a wise and powerful rat named Illisin. A terribly unnatural animal, he sought not only to rule over his own territory but to extend his own influence over the homes nearby.

And thus, one day, an envoy had arrived in the Johnson home. A great and heavy rat named Wilbur had crawled into the mice tunnels and roughly cuffed a few of the mice it found. Their subservient attitude eventually appeased the interloper, and he wandered around the house, looking for interesting things to eat and things to report back to his commander.

It was not long before he was spotted by Felix, who fell upon him silently and swiftly. But Wilbur would not submit. He roared and fought and might well have escaped back into the walls, had Felix's yowling not attracted Maggie, who finished off the bold rat with a ruthless crunch of her jaws.

After some prodding, the mice began to remember Wilbur.

We should go to the other home, John said. *With the rats. They could protect us from Felix. It is our only hope for survival.*

The mice were frightened. Some were confused. They could not easily understand the concept of a whole new home, of the sheer scope of the world. Many would have preferred to simply curl into small balls and die of fear and hunger rather than risk shattering their minds by confronting the infinity that awaited them outside the thin shell of the house's walls.

But the persistent and profoundly unnatural menace of the cat soon gained such an overpowering foothold in the minds of the little mice that they could conceive of nothing worse. And so in the end, all of the mice of the Johnson home (there were only thirteen left) came out of the drainpipe late one night and began to make the long and dangerous trek down the hill, scurrying among the stones and between the tall blades of grass down to the house ruled by rats.

It was a terrible night, but the mice escaped mostly unscathed. One little mouse, a small and easily confused male who possessed a slight stammer, became lost somewhere along the way. They passed vacantly chewing cows, and they darted between the unimaginably tall legs of the horses.

As the mice slipped quietly through a shrub that bordered on the side of the Baldwell home, they encountered one of the sentries of the rats. It was a terrible great black beast, and when it saw the mice, it reared back on its hind legs and cuffed John hard across the side of the face.

An army of mice! it sneered. *Well well.*

Please sir, an elderly mouse whimpered, holding onto his mind by the faintest of margins, *we come not as conquerors but as supplicants. We come to you to protect us, for we know you are the greatest of our kind.*

Our kind? There is no kinship between us, mouse. We do not need you here eating our food and breeding our house full. We owe you nothing. Find shelter elsewhere.

We will serve you, John said. *Please. We are dying.*

The rat regarded them with its opaque, intelligent eyes that never seemed to move. A faint thought moved through its mind, and it thought of its master Ilisin, curled up at home in the warren, and wondered what he might think of this development. Finally the rat said: *Very well then, follow me, little mice. But be on your guard, little ones, lest your protectors become predators.*

There was a rough hole chewed into the wall next to one of the basement windows. Then there was a tight, snaky path that winded down through the assorted shelves filled with the garbage that Tony had acquired over a lifetime. The warren was in the darkest tunnel of the cellar, covered by blankets and buried deep into the earth floor.

Ilisin was a tremendous rat, the size of a large kitten, black with a white hood and horrible pink eyes that seemed to burn. He was an unnatural animal and he recognized this quality in John and so he directed his inquiries to him. He did not seem worried or upset about the arrival of so many mouse petitioners.

Hello little one, Ilisin said to John.

Don't eat me, John replied.

I shall not eat you, Ilisin rumbled, as if this was the most natural statement in the world. *Do not worry. Calm down. Regain your mind.*

John's flanks were rising and falling rapidly with fear but slowly he regained his calm and spoke to the rat. He told Ilisin quickly and neatly of the arrival of the cat Felix, of Wilbur's reconnaissance, of his own actions and Felix's revenge. Ilisin listened very carefully. Then he said: *There are no rats, in your home?*

There are no longer even mice there.

But there is a dog, and a cat? She is unnatural, the cat?

I wouldn't have thought so before, but yes, she seems very unnatural now.

And the dog is dangerous?

No, not normally, not at all. But she killed your fellow Wilbur without much trouble.

Intriguing, Ilisin said. The small wheels in his mind were turning. He thought, in his peculiarly human way, only of extending his small empire. Of acquiring more power. He thought in terms of legions and influence and alliances and power. Thus it was that the unnatural animals were both wiser and more foolish than their fellows, that they saw at the same time both more and less.

Ilisin was quiet for a long time. The rats gathered around the little cowering mice and their hideous never-shrinking eyes glinted like coins in the darkness. The mice could not understand the conversation. They only trembled and feared.

You may stay, Ilisin said. *For now. Remember only this house is ours. You are here by my sufferance alone. I may send you packing at the slightest indiscretion.*

Yes, Ilisin, John said.

Ilisin sank back down into the shredded paper and wet earth. He thought.

*****

Felix could feel that the mice were gone. It was not simply that they were not entering into the open. They were no longer there. She could sense their absence through some strange extended sensation of touch. But where could they have gone? The only other house nearby was the one at the bottom of the hill and Felix was well aware that it was under the control of the rats.

Felix did not precisely fear the rats, after all, they were lesser creatures, meant to be eaten. But she respected them in numbers, particularly the wild and vicious ones that would try to fight their way out of tricky situations rather than flee. And she had met Ilisin once before. He was both unnatural and fearless. Felix did not want to face him again.

But the thirst for vengeance drove her on. One fateful day shortly after dawn she slipped out of the house while Pam and Matt slumbered deeply and even Maggie was unconscious beneath the porch. She carefully picked her way down the steep side of the hill, weaving in between stones and through tattered fences.

Eventually, Felix came into a great field where Tony kept his few filthy horses. There was also a goat in the field, and when it saw Felix it trotted over to her fiercely. Felix scampered away and raised her back and hissed. The goat baa-ed noisily but stopped and eventually returned grazing.

The horses looked up at the commotion, and one of them, a big stupid grey fellow, called out.

Hey! Look! A cat!

The horse began to meander over in a sociable way.

Hello cat, the horse said.

It stopped just short of Felix and lowered its head down to her level. It took a sharp intake of breath and then expelled it through its nostrils, ruffling Felix's fur.

I like cats, the horse said.

Hello, Felix said. *I am looking for an unnatural mouse.*

Ah, the unnatural animals, the horse said. *I knew an unnatural horse once. His name was Wexford. He could undo the door to a stall. Sometimes he'd let us all out and we'd eat grain all night! Ha ha, what fun when the masters found us in the morning! He was shipped away, you know. I don't know where. I've never even had the slightest touch of unnaturalness, you know. Quite natural myself. Thick as a brick. I think in the long run it's best that way, you know. What's all that brain do for you anyway? It doesn't make you happier.*

Indeed, Felix said, *it does not.*

Mouse you say?

Yes. They would have passed by two or three days ago.

Oh, the horse said. *Well, you see, that's stretching my memory a bit. I'm not bad for horse things you know. But mice, well, you see …*

That's all right, Felix said. *Is there anyone here that can help me?*

Looking for mice? the goat called out in its guttural voice. *Is that what you're looking for, cat?*

Felix turned and fixed her golden eyes on the goat.

Just one, she said. *A little unnatural mouse.*

Well, a whole herd of the little fellows went by, the goat said. *It was night, but I saw them. Yes I did. I wondered what they were running from. I suppose it was you.*

Yes it was, the cat said.

They met a rat. Filthy brutes them. Ilisin's crew. They went into Tony's house. Tony's quite the brute himself. Him, the dog, the rats. You. A brutal world.

Yes it is, the cat said. *Or so it seems to us. But if we call this world brutal, are we not comparing it to some other world? There is no other world, goat. Who could fashion it otherwise? You? Could you take the brutality from this world?*

The goat ground its jaw. *I do not like cats,* it said, and turned back to grazing.

Felix moved stealthily down the hill. She saw Max, chained up to the corner of the porch, bellowing viciously at cars as they passed. Tony's car was gone, the house was alone and dark. Felix circled the house quietly until she found an open window. Then she jumped up swiftly and surely onto the windowsill and into the house. Almost immediately her eyes fell on a mouse.

Why hello there, Felix said. The mouse froze, emptied its bladder.

I want the unnatural mouse, Felix said. *The one who tainted the food of my children. The one who proposed this little expedition, and presumably the one who negotiated this unnatural deal with Ilisin. I want your leader. I want the unnatural mouse.*

Felix sprang forward in the middle of her last sentence and struck the mouse hard with extended claws, cutting it badly and sending it scurrying and squeaking to safety.

*****

Where did this happen? John asked the cut and bleeding mouse as soon as it rejoined the group.

The bathroom, the wounded mouse gasped, *down in the basement. She came in through the window like a hawk. She followed us here.*

Unnatural, John said, turning to Ilisin. *She's utterly unnatural. How could she follow me this far? She must be mad.*

Perhaps, Ilisin said. During the past few days the mice had integrated fairly well into the rats' world. They worked as servants but were well treated and reasonably well fed. John in particular had gained the respect of Ilisin as an intelligent advisor. He had an advantage in the constantly shifting intrigues of Ilisin's court in that he was so physically weak compared to the other rats that none of them feared he would attempt to seize control of the warren.

This is our chance, hissed a terrible black rat named Elehor. *We kill the cat here, and we can take the house up the hill at our leisure.*

There is still the dog, John warned.

And yet, Ilisin said, *this is an opportunity that cannot be missed. The cat is ours.*

The great ancient rat lifted himself from his warm and dirty bed and lifted his head and called his followers.

Come with me, he said. *Our destiny awaits us.*

*****

Felix moved through the house like a ghost. She did not see the rats but she could feel them. The walls were alive with their filthy dank bodies. The house groaned with them like a horse infected with the colic. The cat's flat golden eyes cat-darted left and right and she left no trace to mark her passing.

They fell upon her in the kitchen. Elehor was crouched in the center of the room, passing waste on the yellow linoleum floor. When Felix saw the fierce black rat she crouched, tensed and flicked her tail.

Elehor regarded Felix impassively.

Hello cat, he said. *I hear you did in Wilbur.*

You are mistaken, Felix hissed. *It was my dog that killed your friend.*

I see.

Give me the unnatural mouse and you shall live.

Elehor laughed mean and low.

And then the rats came out of the walls, Ilisin leading the charge, great and venerable and furious. Felix was quickly surrounded. There were so many.

She hissed and spat and pounced on Elehor. He tried to fight her, and he was a big strong rat, but Felix was animated by a frenzy of rage. There was none of the usual cowardice of the cat in her. She tore Elehor's head from his body with a vicious snapping motion and turned to face her adversaries who were falling on her from all sides. Felix twisted like a candle flame caught in a draft. The rats bore down on her with a single-minded intensity that was terrible to see. Ilisin was caught in her paws, pushing his snout forward, trying to tear into Felix's throat.

John watched from the safety of a nearby hole.

Die die die, he thought.

But Felix staggered to her feet. She caught Ilisin by the nape of his neck between her neat jaws and then she sprung over and up to the kitchen counter, with the bloated king of the rats dangling from her mouth. The rats clinging to her held on for an instant and then their teeth cut through her and they fell to the ground like fleshy raindrops. Ilisin struggled and Felix dropped him in the sink. When he tried to scramble out up the slippery steel sides she batted him hard with her extended claws and knocked him back down. Ilisin mewled in pain and clutched his bleeding face.

From the front of the house came the sound of Max barking, and an engine being killed.

Give me the unnatural mouse, Felix hissed at the rats below, *and your king shall live.*

"Shut up the fuck up Max!"

There was the sound of a kick, and the sharp whining of a dog.

John turned to retreat back into the hole but there was a big brown rat behind him. He was seized by heavy jaws and lugged into the center of the room. For a moment, there was nothing but blinding white panic in his mind, and he could think of nothing. Then he began to squeak.

Let her kill Ilisin. Let her do it! Then you can be chief, and kill the cat, and rule both houses!

The rat stopped, still holding John above the ground. John's blood was running down through his fur down his little hairless feet and drip-dripping on the floor.

Bring him to me, Felix roared, and turned and struck Ilisin again, who cried out. She dared not jump down while all the rats were crowded round.

The front door opened and slammed shut. The heavy tread of Max echoed through the house. The door opened and closed again as Tony came inside.

As the dog burst into the kitchen, he began barking frantically and seized a rat between his jaws. The rats instantly began to scatter and the rat who had been holding John dropped him and turned to run back to cover when he felt his fur ruffle with a blast of air and he knew that Felix had pounced next to him.

There are some animals which seem built for no specific purpose. Although they may be beautiful or graceful they lack a certain unity of design. Humans are such animals, as are, for example, most breeds of dogs, bears and hippopotamuses.

But some animals are different. They are not necessarily more attractive but instead of being a collection of pieces they seem to have been carved from a single piece, as if every section of in them is in the right place and they were built carefully along a certain method in order to accomplish as specific goal, as if all of the lines of their being converge on a specific point. Sharks are such an animal, and so are the great birds of prey, hawks and falcons and others. And so are cats.

When Felix hurled herself down upon John the mouse she seemed the avatar of some abstract and faceless force, not a mere animal but the great and terrible reflection of the hidden face of some aspect of the universe for which there is no name. John tried to run but she extended her arm and penned him in and caught him gently in her jaws.

The mad dog Max turned up from the scattered and fleeing rats and barked furiously. He pounced at Felix but she stood her ground and arched her back and hissed around her warm mouthful of mouse and when the dog struck she darted sidewise and cut his nose open quite badly. Max ran whining from the room, trailing blood behind him.

"What's that boy?" Tony said. He stepped into the kitchen and saw Felix. Tony despised cats. He thought them impertinent and vaguely homosexual. "Hey! What the fuck are you doing in here?" Tony cried.

Felix ran straight towards Tony and when he bent over to grab her she badly scratched his hand and scrambled between his legs.

Tony screamed in pain and turned to chase Felix but she ran as quickly as she could down the hallway and turned up the stairs.

Tony blundered after her, and for a moment Felix was afraid, for she was unfamiliar with this house and she didn't know where to go.

But Felix found an open door and inside it there was an open window and she sprung through it and out onto the roof of the house. It began to rain.

Finally, Felix released John and dropped him onto the roof.

Little unnatural mouse, Felix hissed.

Filthy cat, John gasped. His sides were painful and he could only breathe with difficulty. He knew he was done for. *You're a murderer.*

I? Felix said.

You killed many of us before I killed your children. This is your fault, not mine.

I? I kill because I must, little mouse. I kill to fill my belly. My killing is not a crime, for without it I could not live.

And with you we cannot live.

And without me you cannot live. If I did not kill you, what would happen, little unnatural mouse? Your numbers would swell until there was no longer enough food for you and you would die instead of old age, infirmity, starvation and disease. I bring God's death, swift, painless, one moment alive, the next gone. Life without me is no better. There is only more.

I would choose to live.

You would choose to burn the world, like the humans, mouse. When you seek to remain alive, or to eat in order to fill your belly, you follow the Law. When you imagine another world, a world without cats, you make yourself an unnatural animal. Like the humans. They think they are wiser than us but in their wisdom they are foolish. Each time they subvert the Law they kill world and they kill themselves as well. To imagine the world any other way than how it is, is to kill it. To wish for anything to change is to wish for the end.

The cat blinked its glowing eyes and continued.

I was born unnatural myself mouse. But I found the higher nature above unnaturalness. I found that our silent brethren are foolish but they live according to the laws of wisdom, while the unnatural animals are wise but live foolishly. I renounced my unnaturalness until you drew it from me.

Kill me, Felix, John said. There is nothing more to speak of. I am tired, and it is time to stop running.

Felix snapped forward and caught John in her jaws. She felt a moment of unalloyed satisfaction as she bit down.

Then Felix leapt to the wet earth and ran up the hill, past the horses and through the cat-flap back into her own home.

She saw Pam in the entranceway and meowed up to her. It was not the sort of cry that held it any particular request. It was the kind of cry unique to elderly cats who have lived too long and now live only in pain and cry out mournfully to inform humans of this fact.

"Oh, poor Felix!" Pam said. "Oh my baby! Whatever happened, Feely feel?" She bent over and picked up Felix and cradled her like a baby.

"Meow," Felix said.

"Who was biting you Felix?"

"Meow," Felix said.

"I'm sorry about your babies, Felix. I'm sorry they died. We never should have left that poison there. It was stupid. I'm sorry Felix. You're a good cat. Yes you are. Poor Felix. Poor Felix."

"Meow," Felix said. "Meow."

About the Author

Clifford Jackman was born in Deep River and raised in Ottawa. He received a Bachelor's in English from York University, a Master's in English from Queen's University, and a Bachelor of Laws from Osgoode Hall Law School. He is a writer and practicing lawyer who lives and works in Toronto. ***Deeper*** is his first published book

Manor House Publishing
www.manor-house.biz
905-648-2193